"You need a lesson in manners."

"Probably. But I also need sex. Are you offering that, too?"

Instead of blushing or throwing her hands up in the air, insulted, she narrowed her eyes. "You could start with introducing yourself—"

"I'm Clint Rockwell. Who are you?" he interrupted her, purely to be ornery.

"Fee...Seraphina Martinez."

Fee suited her, Seraphina didn't.

"You could try speaking in whole sentences, talking to people instead of barking orders at them. And don't get me started on you hauling me around and dumping me like I'm a sack of potatoes."

That mouth. Sassy and made for sex. Talking? Not so much.

"Bring the money to my ranch. Don't make me come looking for you," Clint told her, thinking he'd better leave before he did something stupid, like using his own mouth to cut off her words.

* * *

Rich, Rugged Rancher by Joss Wood is part of the Texas Cattleman's Club: Inheritance series.

Dear Reader,

Welcome to the second book in the Texas Cattleman's Club: Inheritance series!

There are some characters you just fall in love with, and Clint and Fee are my new favorite people. Clint is right up there on my list of the most favorite heroes I've ever created. He's ex-army, has lost his leg, is a little grumpy and a lot sexy, and prefers animals to people. Back in Royal, Texas, he's running his spread and looking after his interest in oil while also being a volunteer fireman. Clint's military and firefighting expertise are going to be needed when a fire ravages the land surrounding Royal.

As for Fee... Well, Fee is a bit of a conundrum. The reality TV star is outspoken, a little in-your-face and a bit of a free spirit. She has a massive heart and while she lives in Manhattan, she knows that she hasn't found the place where she wants to settle down. Having moved all her life with her parents, she doubts she ever will.

Then, she comes to Royal, and she and Clint clash...

I hope you enjoy reading *Rich, Rugged Rancher* as much as I enjoyed writing it. It truly is a book close to my heart.

Happy reading!

Joss

Connect with me on:

Facebook: JossWoodAuthor

Twitter: @JossWoodbooks

Bookbub: Joss-Wood

JOSS WOOD

RICH, RUGGED RANCHER

Special thanks and acknowledgment are given to Joss Wood for her contribution to the Texas Cattleman's Club: Inheritance miniseries

PLEASE RECYCLE
THIS PRODUCT IS RECYCLABLE

Recycling programs for this product may not exist in your area.

ISBN-13: 978-1-335-20883-5

Rich, Rugged Rancher

Copyright © 2020 by Harlequin Books S.A.

Joss Wood loves books and traveling—especially to the wild places of southern Africa and, well, anywhere. She's a wife, a mom to two teenagers and slave to two cats. After a career in local economic development, she now writes full-time. Joss is a member of Romance Writers of America and Romance Writers of South Africa.

Books by Joss Wood

Harlequin Desire

Love in Boston

Friendship on Fire
Hot Christmas Kisses
The Rival's Heir
Second Chance Temptation

Dynasties: Secrets of the A-List

Redeemed by Passion

Texas Cattleman's Club: Inheritance

Rich, Rugged Rancher

Visit her Author Profile page at Harlequin.com, or josswoodbooks.com, for more titles.

You can also find Joss Wood on Facebook, along with other Harlequin Desire authors, at Facebook.com/harlequindesireauthors!

One

"So, have you bagged your cowboy yet?"

Seraphina Martinez whipped the rented convertible onto the open road leading to Blackwood Hollow Ranch and punched the accelerator, ignoring Lulu's squeal of surprise at the sudden burst of speed.

"Slow down, Fee. I don't want to die on a lonely road in East Texas," Lulu grumbled.

"Relax, it's an empty road, Lu," Fee replied, glad she'd wrangled her thick hair into two fat braids—as opposed to Lulu who was fighting, and losing, the war with the wind.

Lulu held her hair back from her face and glared at Fee. "I'm going to look like I've been dragged through a bush when we get there."

Fee shrugged.

Perfect makeup, perfect clothes, perfect hair… being a reality TV star took work, dammit.

"Well, have you?" Fee demanded.

"Found a cowboy? No, not yet," Lulu replied.

"What about the lawyer guy who seems to be everywhere we are lately?" Fee asked. While scouting filming locations for *Secret Lives of NYC Ex-Wives*, the attorney for the Blackwood estate had been everywhere they looked, keeping his lawyerly eye on Miranda Blackwood and the rest of the cast and crew.

"Kace LeBlanc?" Lu asked, aiming for super casual and missing by a mile.

Fee darted a look at her best friend, amused. Of course she had noticed the looks Lulu sent Kace when she didn't think anyone was looking. Lu thought the attorney was hot. And, with his unruly brown hair and those gorgeous brown eyes, he was… until he opened his mouth. Then he acted like she and her costars and the crew were going to break his precious town of Royal or something.

"The guy is a pill," Lulu said before sighing. "God, he's hot but he's so annoying."

Fee agreed but she also admired Kace's determination to look after the late Buck Blackwood's interests and to ensure the terms of his will were followed to the letter. And the terms of the will were, from the little she'd gleaned, astonishing. She couldn't blame his kids for being pissed off at Buck for leaving everything he owned to Fee's co-star Miranda, who was his ex and as New York as she and Lulu were. It had to be a hard slap to their born-and-bred Texas faces.

If they'd scripted this story for *Secret Lives*, their viewers would think they were making it up—aging billionaire leaves much, much younger second wife everything at the expense of his children. Buck also, so she'd heard, had an illegitimate son and this news didn't seem to surprise anyone. Buck, apparently, had liked the ladies.

This plot twist was ratings gold, pure made-for-TV drama.

Lulu looked to her right, her attention captured by a herd of Longhorn cows.

"Did you ever live in Texas?" Lulu asked her, still holding her hair back with two hands.

Fee took some time to answer, trawling through her memories. Being an army brat and having a father who jumped at any chance to move, she'd lived all over the country and attended fourteen schools in twelve years. But she couldn't recall living in Texas.

"I think we did a stint in New Mexico," Fee replied. "But I was young. I don't remember much of it."

Lulu turned in her seat and Fee felt her eyes on her. "I'm still amazed at your excitement over visiting a new place. We've been doing this for years, Fee. Aren't you sick of all the traveling? Don't you miss your own bed?"

Fee sent her a quick smile. "I rent my apartment furnished, Lu. You know that I don't get attached to things or places." She might live in Manhattan but she wasn't as attached to the city as her co-stars were.

"Because you moved so often when you were a child."

"I learned that if you get attached, it hurts like hell when you have to leave." Fee shrugged. "So, it makes sense not to get attached."

"Do you think you'll ever settle down?"

That was a hell of a question. Maybe, possibly, she might one day find a town or city she didn't want to leave. But, because she was a realist, she knew that, while she might stay in a place a couple of months or a few years, she would probably end up moving on. It was what she did.

The grass was always greener around the next corner...

And if you didn't get attached, you couldn't get hurt, especially by people. Her nomadic parents and her own brief marriage to the philandering son of one of NYC's most famous families had taught her that.

She loved people, she did, but underneath her exuberant personality still resided a little girl who knew that relationships (and places) were temporary and believing that any commitment would last was crazy.

She was currently living in Manhattan, in a gorgeous but expensive fully furnished rental in Chelsea. Her practical streak hated the idea of renting when she could easily afford to buy an apartment but Manhattan wasn't a place where she could put down roots. When *Secret Lives* ended, she'd move on, but for now she was comfortable. Not settled but, yeah, temporarily okay with where she laid her head.

She was the captain of her own ship, the author of her own book. And if she was using *Secret Lives* to feather her own nest, to make bank, that was her business. She might be loud, frequently over-the-top, but she was also pragmatic and fully understood how quickly things could change. And if her situation did change—*Secret Lives* was popular now but that could change tomorrow—she wanted her nest to be well feathered.

Because, as she knew, moving from place to place, town to town, wasn't cheap.

And that was why she took every opportunity to maximize her little taste of fame: first with the line of accessories she'd created using her husband's famous last name. Her *Not Your Mama's Cookbook*, written last year, was still on the bestseller lists. Maybe she should think about doing another cookbook…or something else entirely.

It was something to think about.

"Have you decided on your Royal project yet?" Lulu asked her, breaking her train of thought.

"I have no idea what you are talking about," Fee answered, injecting a healthy amount of prim into her tone.

Lulu rolled her eyes. "You can't BS me, Fee. I know it was you who organized giving last season's intern a makeover. Who set Pete, our lighting director, up with Dave, the sound guy. Who read the scriptwriter's—what was his name?—screenplay?

Miranda might be our Mama Bear but you are our Little Miss Fix-It."

Fee wrinkled her nose. Little Miss Fix-It? She opened her mouth to speak then realized she couldn't argue the point. She did tend to identify a need and try to meet it.

"I don't know if I'll find anyone to fix in Royal. I think I'll take a break from meddling while I'm there."

Lulu's laughter danced on the wind. "Yeah, right. That's not going to happen."

Fee frowned at her. "What? I can back off!"

"You cannot!" Lulu retorted. "Honey, we're always getting into trouble because you can't leave a situation alone! We nearly got arrested when you jumped between those two guys fighting in Nero's, and we did get arrested when you—" Lulu bent her fingers to make air quotes "—*confiscated* that abused horse in Kentucky. You are constantly getting trolled on social media because you stand up for LGBT rights, women's rights, immigrants' rights. That's not a criticism, I admire your outspokenness, but you don't have to fight every fight, babe."

Fee knew that. But she also knew what it was like to have no one fighting in her corner, no one to rely on. She knew how it felt to feel invisible and when she stepped out of the shadows, how it felt to be mocked and bullied.

God, she'd come a long way.

"I guarantee you will find a project and you won't

be able to resist meddling," Lulu told her, blue eyes laughing.

"Want to bet?" Fee asked her as they approached the enormous gates to what was Buck Blackwood's—now Miranda's—ranch. The gates to Blackwood Hollow appeared and she flung the car to the right and sped down the long driveway. Lu hissed and Fee grinned.

"What's the bet?" Lulu asked, gripping the armrest with white fingers. "And you drive like a maniac."

"You give me your recipe for Miss Annie's fried chicken for my next cookbook, if I decide to do another one." She'd been trying to pry Lulu's grandma's recipe from her since the first time Lulu fed her the delicious extra-crispy chicken at a small dinner five years earlier.

"She'll come back and haunt me." Lulu gasped, placing her hand on her chest. "I can't. Just like you can't stop yourself from meddling…"

"I can. And you know I can or else you wouldn't be hesitating…"

Lu narrowed her eyes at Fee as they approached a cluster of buildings that looked like a Hollywood vision of a working ranch. A sprawling mansion, guest cottages, massive barns. Despite visiting the spread days before, it was still breathtaking.

"There's the crew's van." Lulu pointed toward the far barn and Fee tapped the accelerator as she drove past the main house that went on and on and on.

"What could be so interesting down by the barns?" Fee wondered.

"That."

Fee looked where Lulu pointed and…holy crispy fried chicken. A man riding a horse at a gallop around a ring shouldn't be a surprise, but what a man and what a horse. Fee didn't know horses—she thought the speckled black-and-white horse might be a stallion—but she did know men.

And the cowboy was one hell of a man. Broad shoulders, muscled thighs, big biceps straining the sleeves of his faded T-shirt. She couldn't see the color of his hair or the lines on his face, the Stetson prevented her from making out the details, but his body was, like the horse, all sleek muscles and contained strength.

Hot, hot, hot…

He also looked familiar. Where did she know him from?

Fee took her foot off the accelerator and allowed the car to roll toward to where the other vehicles—the crew's van, a battered work truck and a spiffy SUV—were parked. All her attention was focused on the horse and rider, perfectly in sync. He seemed oblivious to his audience: a couple of cowboys sitting on the top railing of the fence and Miranda, Rafaela and Zooey standing with their arms on the white pole fence, their attention completely captured by the rider hurtling around the ring in a blur of hooves and dust.

God, he was heading straight for the fence. They'd

either crash through it or he'd have to jump it because there was no way he'd be able to stop the horse in time.

Fee released the wheel and slapped her hands over her mouth, her attention completely caught by the drama in the paddock. She wanted to scream out a warning and was on the point of doing so when the rider yanked on the reins and the stallion braked instantly, stopping when his nose was just an inch from the fence.

That collision didn't happen, but another did when Fee's very expensive rented Audi convertible slammed into the bumper of the battered farm truck.

Lulu released a small shriek and Fee flung her arm out in a futile effort to keep Lulu from lurching forward. Their seat belts kept them in place but metal scraped against metal and steam erupted from her car as the hood got up close and personal with the back of the rust-covered truck.

"Are you okay?" Fee demanded, looking at Lulu.

"Fine," Lulu replied, then winced at the carnage in front of her. "Your car is toast, though—the hood is crumpled."

"I can see that." Fee nodded, releasing her seat belt. "How come it's always the crap cars that sustain the least damage?"

"That crap car is a seventy-two Chevy pickup I am in the process of restoring."

Fee yanked her eyes off Lulu and turned her head to the right, looking straight into faded denim covering strong thighs and a very nice package.

Strong, broad hands rested on his hips, the veins rising on his tanned forearms lightly covered with blond hair. The red T-shirt had faded to orange in places but the chest underneath it was broad and those biceps were big and bitable. His horse—had they jumped the fence to get to her so quickly?—laid its chin on the cowboy's shoulder but neither she, nor the cowboy, were distracted by the animal's interference in their conversation.

Fee kept her focus on him, utterly entranced by his strong face, the blond stubble covering his chiseled jaw, the thin lips, the long, straight nose. The feeling of familiarity coalesced into certainty, she'd seen him before, this cowboy—here at Blackwood Hollow a few days before—but she couldn't recall his name. Probably because he'd just fried most of her brain cells.

She wanted to see his eyes; no, she needed to see his eyes. On impulse, Fee clambered up to stand on her car seat.

God he was tall. Fee pushed the rim of his Stetson up with her finger, her eyes clashing with the deepest, saddest, green-gold-gray eyes.

Hard eyes, angry eyes, sad, sad eyes.

Fee couldn't decide what she wanted to do more, hug him or jump him.

Save the horse and ride the cowboy, indeed.

Clint Rockwell was a guy of few words but if Buck Blackwood were magically resurrected, he'd have had more than a few to hurl at his friend and mentor's head. What the hell had he been thinking to ask Clint to mind the property during his long illness and after his death?

Since Buck's funeral, Clint had been coming over to Blackwood Hollow a few times a week, to check on the hands and to exercise Buck's demon horse, Jack.

He and Jack were finally starting to bond and their skills were improving. Clint lifted his hand to hold Jack's cheek, enjoying the puffs of horse breath against his neck.

Animals were cool; people were not.

People hurt people—and sometimes things, his pickup being a case in point. Ignoring Jack, Clint walked over to the hood of the Audi convertible and dropped to his haunches to inspect the damage to his pickup. He didn't much care about the damage to the convertible, they were dime a dozen, but his truck was vintage and worth a pretty penny.

Hey, Rock, if I don't make it, finish my truck for me. Only original parts, man, gold and cream.

You are going to make it because if you don't, I'm going to paint it pink and white, Clint had told him, his hand in the hole in Tim's chest, trying to stem the river of blood soaking his hand, Tim's clothing and the dirt road beneath them.

They'd both known Clint's optimism was a lie, that Tim needed blood and a surgeon and that he was out of time.

I'll haunt you if you do anything stupid to my baby, Tim had muttered.

This accident probably qualified as a haunting.

Hell, Clint didn't sleep anyway, so Tim was welcome to pop in for a chat. His army ranger buddies were the only people Clint liked being around for any length of time, the only people on the planet who understood. They'd seen what he had, had watched men they loved be blown apart, women and children die, buildings being ravaged and lives destroyed.

They got him.

Civilians didn't.

Oh, the people in this town tried, sure. No man with his money and property ever had to be lonely if he didn't want to be. He wanted to be. His army days were behind him and he was now a rancher and oilman—more rancher than oilman, truth be told. His land and animals were what mattered.

Shaking off his thoughts, Clint stood up, automatically using his good leg to take his weight. He had to stop doing that; he had to start treating his prosthetic as another leg but, shit, it was hard. Leaving the force had been hard, losing a limb had nearly killed him and being forced to deal with people, civilians, was the cherry on his crap sundae.

Clint turned and cursed when he saw he was the focus of much attention and quickly, and automatically, took in all the salient details. Since he was still ignoring the driver of the convertible—he wasn't ready to deal with her yet—he turned his attention to the passenger. Sporting glossy black hair with dark eyes, she'd left the car and was standing with Miranda Blackwood, Buck's ex-wife. With them was also a fresh-faced beauty and an Italian bombshell who reminded him of one of Grandpa's favorite actresses, Sophia Loren.

The four women, Buck's ex-wife and her reality TV co-stars, watched him with avid interest. They looked as out of place as he would on a catwalk, their spiked heels digging into the grass, designer sunglasses covering their eyes.

The Blackwood ranch hands couldn't keep their eyes off them…

He uttered a low, sharp order for them to get back to work and they hopped off the fence with alacrity, tossing admiring looks at the New Yorkers as they ambled off.

The next problem was to get the cars untangled so he could accurately assess the damage to Tim's truck. But first he had to take care of Jack: animals first, things later.

Clint called out to a hand and when he jogged back to where Clint was standing, Clint passed him Jack's reins. "Can you cool him down, then brush him for me?"

"Sure, boss."

Clint didn't correct him since he was, by Buck's decree, the temporary boss. And ordering people around wasn't something new to him; he'd been the owner–operator of Rockwell Ranch since he was eighteen and a lieutenant in Delta Force. Despite their enormous wealth, thanks to ranching and business acumen and large deposits of oil, serving was family tradition: his great grandfather saw action in

France in 1917, his grandfather fought the Japanese in the Philippines. His father did two years in the military but never saw any action. His dad didn't see much of anything, having died shortly before Clint's fifth birthday.

Anyway, it felt natural to join the army, and then it felt natural to become one of the best of the best.

Excellence was what he did.

Jack stepped on his foot as he walked away— bastard horse—and Clint didn't react. If he'd been alone, he'd have told Jack he'd lost his leg above the knee and having his foot stood on barely registered on his pain-o-meter but there were people about. He never discussed his prosthetic leg, ever.

Mostly because he was allergic to pity and he was terrified of people thinking he was weak. He might be half the man he'd once been but he'd rather die than allow people to coddle him.

He didn't need anybody or anything…not anymore.

But he did need this damn car moved.

"Look, I'm sorry, I lost focus."

She sounded more defensive than sorry, Clint decided as he walked back to the driver's door of the Audi. The driver was now sitting on the top of the front seat, brand-new cowboy boots on the white leather. Clint started there, at those feet, and slowly made his way upward. Now that the red haze had lifted from his vision—he was still mad as hell but he was in control—he could take in the details.

Holy crap…

Slim legs in skin-tight blue jeans, curvy hips and a teeny waist he was sure he could span with his hands. She wore a lacy, button-down shirt and a heap of funky necklaces. Two thick braids, deep brown at the top and lighter at the ends, rested on a fantastic pair of breasts.

He lifted his eyes to her face, his mouth dry. Yep, she had a rocking body but her face was 100 percent gorgeous. A stubborn chin, a mouth made for kissing, high cheekbones and merry, mischievous, naughty eyes—deep brown—framed by long, long lashes and a cocky pair of eyebrows.

A straw Stetson covered her head.

She might be pint-sized but Clint just knew every inch of her was trouble

He jerked his head sharply. "Move."

She cocked her head and sent him a slow smile. "No."

Okay, admittedly he hadn't had a lot of interaction with people lately but when he used his don't-mess-with-me voice, people generally hustled. "What?"

"Say please."

Clint stared at her, not sure he'd heard her correctly. Shaking his head, he tried again. "Lady, move."

The smile grew sweeter. And deadlier. "No."

What the everlasting…

"Have you heard of the phrases *please* and *thank you*?" she asked, cocking her head.

She was lecturing him on manners? She'd dinged his truck, probably putting back his restoration by months and months, had barely apologized herself and then had the balls to throw his manners in his face?

Red haze descending again, he didn't trust himself to speak so Clint took the next easiest option. Stepping up to the car, he swiftly slid one arm under her knees, the other around her slim back and swung her off her perch.

But instead of placing her feet on the ground, he held her to his chest, fighting the wave of lust running through him. There was something about the soft, fragrant give of a woman, the curve of her hip beneath his fingers, the softness of her breast pushing into his chest. Her minty breath, the surprise in those deep dark eyes.

Soft, sexy lips he desperately wanted to taste…

God, he needed sex. It had been a while…another thing that changed when he lost his leg. He hated pity, from others and loathed a woe-is-me attitude but experience had taught him that normal women, women who weren't loons and gold diggers, weren't crazy about one one-legged guys with too many scars to count. His girlfriend sure as hell hadn't.

"So, this is comfortable," she purred, looking as relaxed as if she was stretched out on a lounger by a sparkling pool, margarita in her hand.

Did anything faze her?

Wanting to find out, Clint loosened his grip on her and she fell a few inches before he caught her again. Instead of squealing she just tightened her arms around his neck and those eyes, the color of his favorite dark chocolate, met his. "You wouldn't drop me."

"Watch me." Knowing there was a half decimated, now loosely packed hay bale behind him, he whipped her around and released her. Her face reflected her horror and anger as she braced to hit the hard ground. When her pretty butt landed on the hay, her eyes widened and her comical what-just-happened expression almost made him smile.

But he didn't. Because smiling wasn't something he did anymore.

Pulling his eyes off his faux cowgirl, he hopped into the convertible, cranked the engine and released the brake. Slapping the car into Reverse, he pulled away from his truck and stared down at the dashboard, noticing the flashing warning lights. Water, oil, temperature were all going nuts. Yep, she wasn't going anywhere, anytime soon.

Not his problem…

Clint cut the engine and exited the car. Ignoring the tiny woman who was trying to extract herself from the inside of the hay bale, he walked over to his truck and slapped his hand on his hip. It wasn't as bad as he'd feared. The tailgate was damaged but he was pretty sure he could find another. The lights were broken but he knew a guy who had spares. It would cost him but he could afford to pay for the damage.

Actually, he should just get the peanut to pay. Judging by the rocking diamond ring on her right hand and the fat diamond studs she wore in her ears, she could afford to pay the bill out of pocket rather than forcing him to haggle with an insurance agency.

He tossed a look over his shoulder at her. "I expect you to pay for the repairs. Twenty grand should cover it." Twenty thousand was ten times more than he needed but he figured she should pay for inconveniencing him. "I don't want to wait for the insurance company, so you can pay me and fight with them."

Her head jerked up and she pushed up the brim of her cowboy hat to glare at him. "What?"

"I want twenty K. Preferably in cash."

Those eyes hardened. "Are you off your meds? I'm not paying you twenty grand! You could buy a new truck for less than that."

Sure, but could he buy a 1972 Chevy pickup with an original, hardly used engine, original seats and fixtures? Not damn likely.

"You can find me at Rockwell Ranch. Don't make me come looking for you," Clint warned her as he walked around the hood of his truck to the driver's door. He climbed in, grabbing the steering wheel and pulling himself up, his upper body strength compensating for his missing limb. Slamming the door closed, he rested his arm on the window, surprised to see she was still glaring at him, utterly unintimidated.

Now that was a surprise because Clint knew his hard face, gruff voice and taciturn attitude scared most people off.

Instead of being frightened, she stomped over to him, pieces of hay stuck in her braid. Intrigued to see what she would do, or say, he held her hot gaze.

"You need a lesson in manners."

"Probably. I also need sex. Are you offering that too?"

Instead of blushing or throwing her hands up in the air, insulted, she narrowed her eyes. "In your dreams, cowboy. Who do you think—"

"Who are you?" he interrupted her, purely to be ornery.

"Fee… Seraphina Martinez."

Fee suited her. Seraphina didn't.

And that mouth. It was sassy and sensuous and made for sex. Talking? Not so much.

"Bring the money to my ranch—don't make me come looking for you," Clint told her, thinking he'd better leave before he did something stupid, like using his own mouth to cut off the tirade that was, obviously, coming.

Shit, he was losing it.

"I'm ten miles down the road. You'll see the gates." Clint cranked the engine and placed his hand on the gear stick. He tapped his Stetson with two fingers.

"Ma'am," he said, purely to irritate her.

Annoyance and frustration jumped into her eyes. "Don't you 'ma'am' me! I *will* get you to learn some manners."

Hell, if she was under him, naked, he'd learn anything she wanted him to. *Enough now, Rock, drive off.*

"Honey, I don't do people so I don't do manners. I just need my twenty K."

"When pigs fly," Fee muttered, her hands on

those curvy hips. Clint looked at her mouth again and fought the urge to leave the car, haul her into his arms and taste it. To inhale her sweet scent and pull her into his—he looked down—rock-hard erection.

Over the roar of his engine, he heard one of the women shout across to the fake cowgirl. "Is he going to be your next project, Fee?"

Fee looked at him and her smile chilled him to his core. "You know what? I rather think he is."

What the hell did she mean by that?

Time to go.

Clint slammed his pickup into Reverse, conscious that all the New Yorkers were still staring at him. But he only wanted to see the brunette with the smart mouth and tempting curves in his rearview mirror. She was sexy as hell and, because he wasn't a total idiot, he'd noticed her attraction to him.

Clint barreled down the driveway and tossed his Stetson onto the empty seat next to him. He'd seen her checking him out and suspected she liked what she'd seen, up to a point. He'd worked hella hard to build his core, chest and back muscles. Women liked his top half but, these days, his bottom half caused him problems.

Hell, both the women—his mom and his girl-friend—he'd ever loved had been unable to come to terms with his disability...

The memories rolled back and Clint forced himself to face them. On returning from Afghanistan, he'd spent a couple of months in hospital recovering after his amputation and when he got back to the ranch, he'd spent a few more months in bed, sleeping and smoking and drinking.

Carla, his long-time girlfriend, had immediately moved in to take care of him and she'd run around, waiting on him hand and foot. It didn't matter to her that he could afford to hire teams of nurses, doctors and physiotherapists. Family money, lots and lots of money, gave him access to the best health care on the planet but Carla only allowed the bare minimum of people to have access to him.

She'd insisted on fussing over him herself, coddling and mothering him. But, as his depression lifted, he realized that he didn't like the flabby, bloated, unhealthy man he saw in the mirror. He'd always been a fitness fanatic and because he was sick of feeling sick and miserable, he turned two rooms of his ranch house into a state-of-the-art gym.

As he got fitter, and more adept with his prosthetic, he became more independent and Carla had mentally, and physically, retreated. And when his sex drive finally returned, she'd retreated some more. When he'd finally convinced her that he was well enough, strong enough, for sex and taken his prosthetic off, she bolted.

Never to be seen again.

Thanks to his frequent absences due to his career in the military, they'd drifted apart and his accident pulled them back together again. She adored his dependence on her, loved being so very needed and had he stayed that way, she might've stuck around. But being weak wasn't something Clint did. Weakness wasn't part of his DNA.

His sex life didn't improve after she left. He'd tried a couple of one-night stands and neither were successful. One woman left when she saw his leg, another, the next morning, acted like she'd done him the biggest favor by sleeping with him and Clint decided that climaxes with strangers weren't worth the humiliation.

It had been two years since he got laid and, yeah, he missed sex. And when he met someone he was instantly, ridiculously attracted to, as he'd been to that brunette back there, he missed it more than ever.

But sex was just sex; he wouldn't die from not getting any.

He didn't think.

Clint felt his phone vibrating in the back pocket of his jeans and lifted his butt cheek to pull it out. Glancing down at the screen, he saw the Dallas area code and recognized the number as one of his mother's.

The mother he no longer spoke to.

Clint briefly wondered why she, or more likely her PA or another lackey, was calling. It had been years since they'd last spoken but he didn't answer the call. He had nothing to say to his mom. Not anymore...

Mila had blown into the hospital to visit with him before his operation and he'd been cynically surprised by her show of support as she'd never been an attentive, involved mother.

Back in his room after the operation that took his leg, he'd hadn't felt strong enough to deal with his intense news-anchor mother and he'd pretended to still be under the anesthetic, hoping she'd go away. He'd just wanted the world to leave him alone but his hearing hadn't disappeared along with his leg and Mila's softly spoken words drifted over to him.

So, I'm here, he's still out so what now?

I've arranged for the press to photograph you leaving the hospital after visiting your war-hero son. Clint had recognized the voice as Greg's, Mila's business manager, whom he'd met a few times over the years. He was, so Mila said, the power behind Mila's rise to being one of the most famous, powerful and respected women in Dallas.

So, try to look worried, distressed. And proud.

I'm going to have to act my ass off, Mila had moaned. *He's, like...repulsive.*

Jesus, Mila, he's your son, Greg had said, sounding, to his credit, horrified.

I like pretty and I like perfect. He's never been perfect but before he went off to play at war, he was at least pretty, Mila had retorted. *Thank God he has that girlfriend because I'm certainly not prepared to be his nurse.*

Wow. Her words laid down just another hot layer of pain.

With her words bouncing off his brain, Clint had slipped into sleep and a six-month depression. Carla and his mother were the reasons he'd worked his butt off to become, as much as possible, the person he was before the surgery. He never wanted to be dependent on anyone ever again, not for help, sex or even company. Carla had wanted to help him too much, his mother not at all, but Clint was happy to be shot of them both.

All he wanted was for the few people he chose to interact with to see past his injury to the man he was. And he couldn't do that if he flaunted his prosthetic so he never, ever allowed anyone to see his bionic leg.

And if giving up sex was the price he paid for his independence then he'd happily live with the lack of below-the-belt action. Nothing was more important to him than his independence. And his pride.

But some days, like today, a woman came along who made him wonder, who made him burn. But he was nothing if not single-minded, and like the others he'd felt a fleeting attraction to, he wouldn't act on it.

No woman was ever worth the hassle.

Two

Fee slid into a booth in Royal's diner and nodded her appreciation. Every time she walked through the doors, she had the same thought: that this was what a diner should look like: 1950s-style decor, red fake-leather booths, black-and-white checkerboard linoleum floor and the suggestion that gossip flowed through here like a river.

She rather liked Royal, Texas. It was, obviously, everything New York City wasn't—a slow-paced small town with space to breathe.

From being yanked from town to town with her parents, Fee had honed the ability to immediately discern whether a town would, temporarily, suit her or not. She'd hated Honolulu—weird, right?—and loved Pensacola, tolerated Tacoma and loved

Charleston. But something about Royal called to her; she felt at ease here.

She would never belong anywhere—Manhattan was where she'd chosen to work and socialize but it still wasn't home, she didn't think any place would be—but Royal was intriguing.

Strange that this small town with its wide, clean streets and eclectic mix of people and shops was where she felt more relaxed than she had in a long, long time.

Fee grinned. If she kept on this mental train, soon she would be thinking she could live on a ranch and raise cows. She snorted and looked down at her manicured fingers and soft hands. This from a girl who believed meat came from the supermarket and eggs from cardboard cartons?

Now, crotchety Clint Rockwell looked like he was born to ride the range. The man was one sexy cowboy. Pity he had the personality of a rabid raccoon. Fee put her hand on the box lying on the table and grinned.

Twenty thousand to fix a heap of rust? Ok, that wasn't fair, it was vintage truck and probably rare but the repair, from her research, wouldn't cost that much! She knew she was being hustled; she wasn't the village idiot.

Well, she might be a reality TV star but she was a pragmatic reality TV star and she didn't hand out money like it was M&M's.

If he hadn't been such a snot she might've tossed in a few extra grand to compensate him for the inconvenience but the guy had taken jerk to a whole new level…

He needed to be brought down a peg or six.

Fee heard the door to the diner swing open and watched as Lulu threaded her way through the tables to fall into the seat opposite her. Like her, Lulu had also dressed down in jeans. In her case, they were topped with a simple white, thigh-length jersey, a brightly colored scarf in a complicated knot around her neck. Lu slapped a paper folder on the table between them and frowned at the board game Fee had purchased from the toy shop down the road. It was a game to teach kids about money and, importantly, the notes inside looked remarkably real.

"I'm sure we can find something to do in Royal that doesn't include board games," Lulu stated.

Fee grinned. "I'm not playing with you. I'm going to play with someone else."

"You're going to pay him in toy money?" Lulu caught on instantly. That was one of the many reasons they were best friends. "Oh, clever."

Fee put her hands together as if to pray and bowed her head. "Thank you. Did the *Secret Lives* researcher dig up any information on Clint Rockwell?" she demanded, pulling the folder to her. "I mean, I don't think he's one of Royal's leading lights—not with a personality like his—but maybe he made the papers because he did something stupid. I can see him busting up a bar or racking up speeding tickets, maybe breaking and entering…"

"You have a hell of an imagination," Lulu commented, thanking the waitress when she offered coffee.

Fee was certain that Clint Rockwell was not the boy next door, not someone who was part of the Chamber of Commerce or a member of the illustrious Texas Cattleman's Club.

He was an outsider, a loner, someone who didn't do group events. Someone mysterious, possibly dangerous…

Fee flipped open the folder and looked down to see a photograph of Rockwell looking very un-farmy. In this photograph, his short dark-blond hair was covered by a tan beret immediately identifying him as an army ranger. He wore a dark blue dress uniform with about a million medals on his chest, including a Purple Heart.

Well, she'd gotten one thing right—as part of that elite regiment, he was definitely dangerous.

Fee was about to move the photograph to the side when she heard the waitress sigh. Fee looked up to find the young girl's eyes firmly on the photograph. Fee couldn't blame her for taking a moment. Rockwell, looking like Captain America in his dress blues, was definitely sigh worthy.

"It's so sad."

Fee exchanged a look with Lulu and frowned. "What's so sad?" Lulu asked the waitress, whose name tag stated she was Julie.

Julie gestured to the photograph with her coffee carafe. "Clint Rockwell. Poor guy."

Ooh, gossip. Fee leaned back, her full attention on the waitress. "Why? What happened to him?"

"He's a Rockwell, so obviously there's no shortage of cash. Like his daddy, his granddaddy and his granddaddy before him, Clint is an oilman and a rancher. But he leases his oil fields and occupies himself with his ranch. And with coordinating Royal's volunteer fire department."

Fee's head spun with all the information. She held up a hand. "He's a fireman too?"

"Apparently, he did some firefighting course in California before he enlisted." Julie pulled her eyebrows together, looking a little confused. "Where was I? Right, his daddy died when he was young, really young, and he and his mama don't talk."

Yeah, that was sad. Her parents might have hauled her from pillar to post and back to pillar but they were now settled in Florida and she saw them occasionally. In fact, she was heading there shortly to spend Christmas with them. They weren't super close but she knew she was loved, in an abstract kind of way.

"The Rockwells are a Royal institution, a founding family and really rich."

"How rich?" Fee asked, as direct as always.

"Mega," Julie replied.

And he was stiffing her for twenty grand? The bastard!

"What else can you tell me about him?" Fee asked, her temper bubbling.

"He lost his leg in a helicopter crash. That's how

he earned his Purple Heart. His leg was mangled. His whole unit was seriously injured. Apparently, the helicopter crashed in an enemy-controlled area and he, and another guy, held off the bad guys until reinforcements arrived. Half of his unit survived, but Clint lost his leg."

Fee frowned at Julie, not understanding. "He lost his leg?" She'd noticed he walked with a slight limp but never suspected he wore a prosthetic.

Julie nodded. "Yeah. That's why he left the army." Julie shrugged. "Ever since he got back, he's become a bit of a recluse and doesn't have much to do with Royal residents, except for the volunteer firefighters. And he never, ever talks about his tours, his regiment or his injury. Like, *ever*."

Someone called Julie and she sent them an apologetic smile. "Sorry, got to go."

Fee transferred her gaze to Lulu, who looked equally disbelieving. "He's disabled?"

"He looked plenty abled," Fee replied. "I would never have thought…"

"Holy crap." Lulu rested her hand on her heart. "Hot, brave and sexy—I think I might be a little in love with him."

Fee felt a surge of jealousy and did an internal eye roll. What was wrong with her? Flipping the folder closed—why had they sent the researcher to the local library when the source of good information could be pumped for details over coffee?—Fee stared out of the window and watched the activity on the street outside.

Did this information change anything? She was as much a sucker for a wounded war hero as the next person and she had a million questions. Why was he a loner? How had he managed to master his prosthetic leg to be able to ride as he did? Why was he holding her up for twenty grand if he was loaded? But mostly, she just needed to figure out whether this changed her plans.

If he hadn't lost his leg, she wouldn't have hesitated to confront him and toss the fake money in his face. But should this revelation really hold her back? Her thinking she should go easy on him because he'd lost a leg was insulting in the extreme. He'd already proven he could more than handle her, and lost leg or not, the guy needed to learn some manners.

"You're still going to confront him," Lulu stated, sounding resigned.

"Damn straight I am."

"He's pretty intimidating, Fee," Lulu said, concern in her voice. "I'm not sure whether you should go out to his ranch alone."

Fee instinctively shook her head. "He's not going to hurt me, Lu. Oh, his tongue might raise some blisters, but he'd never raise a hand to me."

"How do you know?"

Fee lifted both shoulders and ran her hand through her hair. "I have a strong gut feeling about him. He's not dangerous…sad, confused, bitter, sure. But he won't hurt me."

Lulu sighed. "And you see his lack of manners and his rudeness as a challenge."

"Sure. Someone needs to set him straight. I'm sorry he lost a leg but it doesn't give him the right to act like an ass."

Lulu pinned her to her seat with hard eyes. "Oh, I know you, Seraphina Martinez—and I know what this is really about. Yes, bad manners and rudeness annoy you, but you also see him as a challenge. You want to know if you can be the one who can break through to him, make him more sociable."

Fee avoided eye contact, waiting for Lulu to drop the topic. But her friend wasn't done.

"I don't think he's going to like being one of your projects, Fee," Lulu told her, worry coating every word. "He's not going to bend under the force of your personality and if he wanted friends, he would make his own. You don't need to rescue every stray who comes across your path, Seraphina."

Lulu's use of her full name was a solid clue to her seriousness. Fee wrinkled her nose. "Do I really do that?"

"You know you do! You have the strongest rescue gene of anyone I know! He's a veteran, you have a soft spot for soldiers because you grew up on an army base. Add hero and wounded to the mix and you want to wrap him up in a blanket and coddle him."

"I'd rather unwrap him and do him," Fee admitted. She pulled a face and forced the words out. "I'm crazy attracted to him, Lu."

"Any woman, and more than a few guys, would be," Lulu replied. "And that's okay. Although you're not big on one-night stands or brief flings, if you want to sleep with him, do. But when he puts his clothes back on, don't try to fix him, Fee. Respect his right to be alone, to choose how he interacts with the world. From the sound of it, he's gone through hell and back. If he wants to be left alone, he's earned the right." Lulu gripped her hand and continued. "Fixing him might make you feel better but it's not about you, it's about him."

Lu's words smacked her in the chest. She stared down at the folder, her breath a little ragged. She did like the feeling of accomplishment she got when she managed to solve someone else's problems. Sometimes it felt like she was filling in pieces of herself. But Lu was right, this wasn't a makeover, or a blind date, or a rescued horse. This was a man of pride, honor and discipline who'd served his country with distinction. He'd trained hard, sacrificed much, seen and experienced situations no one should have to see and she had no right to make judgments about his life. Or to presume she knew what was best for him.

Fee pulled in a deep breath and met Lulu's eyes. "Okay."

"Okay…what?"

"Okay, I won't try to fix him, to rescue him from his lonely life," Fee clarified. "But I *am* going to confront him about his rudeness and his lack of manners. You can be a hermit without being an ass."

Lulu slapped her hand against her forehead and groaned. "And are you still going to pay him off with toy money?"

Fee nodded. "Damn right I am."

"And are you going to sleep with him?"

She couldn't lie, she was very tempted. Fee lifted one shoulder and both her hands. "He's tempting, so tempting, and I shouldn't…"

"But?"

Fee didn't want to be attracted to him, and as God and Lulu knew, she wasn't in the habit of falling into bed with guys on a whim—or at all—but she didn't think she could resist the sexy, sad, rude cowboy. "But if he asks me, I just might."

Clint hated surprise visitors—he never wanted to be caught without his prosthetic or using crutches—so he'd installed cameras all over the ranch and had them wirelessly connected so they sent an alert to his phone whenever he had company. He grabbed his cell from the back pocket of his jeans, pulled up the screen connecting him to his camera feed and saw another convertible—red, this time—flying up his driveway.

Yep, she was back.

Clint, walking a mare that had colic, whistled and when Darren's head popped out from a stall, he jerked his head. "Can you carry on walking Belle for me?"

Darren's eyes widened with concern. "LT, I have no experience with horses and this one is, so I hear, one of your best."

Clint smiled at the familiar nickname for *lieutenant*. "It's just walking, Darren, and we're civilians now—you can call me Clint. If you run into trouble with her or you think something is wrong, just yell for Brad. He'll hear you and take over."

Brad, his foreman, didn't always agree with his policy of hiring out-of-work veterans instead of experienced hands but Clint insisted that learning to muck out stalls and fix fences didn't require experience. The ranch needed people who wanted to work and there were so many vets needing to find a way to support themselves and their families.

And, as he knew, open skies, fresh air and animals were a great way to deal with the memories of war.

"I'll be back as soon as I can."

Darren nodded, took the reins and led the horse to the entrance of the stable. Clint broke into a jog, heading for his dirt bike parked just outside. Gunning the accelerator, he headed back to his house, cutting around the back of the stables to arrive at the main house at the same time she did.

They both cut their engines at the same time and Clint rested his forearms on the handlebars of his bike, watching her from behind his dark glasses and the brim of his Stetson. The sun was starting to dip and he could probably ditch both but they provided a shield he badly needed...

He couldn't let her know how attracted he was to her, how he wanted nothing more than to take her inside and get her naked and horizontal.

Actually, he just needed her naked because vertical worked too.

Clint watched as she shoved an expensive pair

of designer shades into her hair, the arms raking her loose curls off her face. She wore less makeup today than she had yesterday. Her lips were a pale pink instead of bright red and her outfit consisted of a cranberry-colored jersey that worked well with her creamy skin and those brilliant dark eyes.

God, she was hot. He couldn't invite her into the house: first, because his crutches were leaning against the wall in the hallway—he'd put on his leg while sitting on the bench in the hallway early this morning—and second because he wasn't sure he could resist her.

Fee opened the door of the rental and climbed out, shapely legs in tight blue jeans tucked into low-heeled, knee-high boots. The jersey clung to her breasts and curves of her hips and Clint felt all the moisture leave his mouth.

He'd stormed houses filled with terrorists in Afghanistan, had faced down a Somalian warlord and protected his guys while they waited for an evac after the crash but he'd never experienced such a dry mouth.

But this woman, with her black-brown hair and expressive eyes, managed to achieve what a dozen treacherous situations hadn't...

And that scared the crap out of him, which added another layer to his grouch.

"Have you got my money?" he demanded, staying where he was.

"Hello, Fee, how are you? Did you find the place

okay?" Fee singsonged, calling attention yet again to his lack of manners.

Tough. He didn't have the time and energy to play nice; he just wanted her to be gone before he made a stupid suggestion like, "Let's go to bed."

Because that was a disaster waiting to happen. He'd have to explain he was missing a limb and then, if she didn't rabbit, he'd have to wait and see if she could deal with his stump and scars.

Such fun…

Nope, it was a game he was better off not playing.

"You're wasting my time, Martinez," Clint warned, dismounting the bike and pocketing the keys. He waited for her at the bottom of the stairs leading up to his wraparound porch and the front door. He wouldn't invite her inside but they could, at least, get out of the sun.

Instead of following him, Fee placed her hands on her hips and tipped her head back to look at the house he still thought of as his Grandpa's—the place where he'd visited the family patriarch every summer from the time of his dad's death when Clint was five until he turned eighteen and enlisted.

At the time he hadn't cared where the army sent him, as long as it kept him away from his mother's hounding to study law or something equally boring. He couldn't have known that shortly after he enlisted, his beloved grandpa would die, and Clint would become the fifth Rockwell to own the land.

Grandpa Rockwell always said that he didn't want the land to be a burden, to be a noose around his neck. He'd been the biggest supporter of his military career so Clint hadn't felt the need to rush home when he died, comfortable to place the ranch in Brad's capable hands until his return.

He'd always preferred the ranching side of his inheritance so he'd leased his oil fields. Years later, he was still happy for someone else to deal with that side of the business.

"I like your house," Fee said, and he frowned at the note of surprise in her voice. "It's big, obviously, like everything else in Texas, but it's not ostentatious. I don't do ostentatious."

"Says the girl driving another fast, expensive convertible," he drawled.

Fee looked back at the car and her husky laughter surprised him. "Touché. But I'm a real gearhead and I don't get to drive as often as I'd like to."

"I'm sure all the residents of New York City are eternally grateful for that fact, because you have a lead foot," Clint said. "And how did you charm the rental company into trusting you with another fast car after your crash yesterday?"

"I apologized sincerely and asked them nicely," Fee retorted, her eyes flashing with irritation.

"You didn't apologize to me," Clint pointed out.

"I tried to! But then you started barking orders and tossing me into hay bales!"

Clint lifted his index finger. "One. One hay bale."

Fee rolled her eyes. "Whatever… Anyway, you should try this thing called charm or, this is a radical idea so beware, a smile. Oh, your face might crack but I think you'll survive the experience."

Clint felt the corner of his mouth twitch with amusement. He loved her sassy mouth and now rather liked the fact that he didn't intimidate her. He walked up onto the porch and gestured to a cluster of outdoor furniture to the left of the door.

"Take a seat."

Fee's winged eyebrows shot up. "Ooh, manners. There's hope for you yet."

"Don't bet on it," Clint replied, putting his hands into the back pockets of his jeans. He watched as she sat on the arm of one wicker chair, casually draping one gorgeous leg over the other and tucking her foot behind her calf. Such a female, sexy movement, full of grace and charm.

Clint waited her out, knowing silence was usually a good way to hurry the conversation along by forcing the other person to talk. But Fee confounded him again by ignoring his scowl and silence, seemingly content to watch the mares frolicking in the paddock closest to the house.

Why couldn't this woman do what he expected her to?

Clint rocked on his heels, his eyes constantly dropping to her lips, wondering whether she tasted as spicy as she sounded. He eventually broke their silence. "Why are you here, Seraphina?"

Fee flashed a smile and leaned down to tuck her hand into her very large leather bag—big enough to carry a change of clothes, a bag of groceries and a saddle or two—and pulled out a couple of rolls of cash. He saw a fifty-dollar bill under the rubber band of one and a hundred-dollar bill around the other. He sucked in his breath.

He'd been annoyed yesterday and tossed out twenty thousand as a figure, hoping to annoy her. But, judging by the cash she'd brought along, she'd taken him seriously.

He couldn't take her money, not now and not ever.

Clint was about to tell her to put it away when he noticed the rolls seemed irregular, that not all the edges of the bills lined up. If he hadn't been so distracted by her, he would've immediately noticed that something was wrong with the roll, that her sweet, innocent expression was as fake as hell.

Oh, hell no, she wouldn't dare…

He held out his hand and instead of handing the first one over, she threw it at his chest. He caught the first one, then the second and tucked it under his arm, snapping the rubber band off the first.

Yep, as he thought. A real note covering fake money. Toy money…

Clint felt a bubble of laughter rise within him, tried to swallow it and failed. When his husky-from-lack-of-use chuckle filled the space between them, he was as surprised as Fee.

He couldn't remember the last time he'd laughed…

He heard Fee's smothered laugh, a cross between a hiccup and a giggle. And because he wanted to taste his laughter on her lips, because he wanted to taste her, Clint moved quickly and, after placing his hands on either side of the arm of the chair, bent down and kissed her.

And immediately wished he hadn't.

Because, as their lips touched, as her mouth opened and her fingers came up to touch the scruff on his jaw, he knew he'd never be satisfied with just one kiss…

He wanted more. Much, much more.

He was a grouch and a grump, curmudgeonly and contrary, but hellfire, the man could kiss. Fee found herself surging to her feet, her arms looping around his neck, her breasts pushing into his chest. She felt his big hand on the top of her butt, pulling her into a very thick, concrete-hard erection, and she whimpered in delight.

He was so big, everywhere. Fee found herself on her tiptoes, straining to align their mouths, knowing they'd both have cricks in their necks at the end of this make-out session. Clint solved the problem by placing his hands on her hips and boosting her up against his body, holding her weight with ease. What else was a girl to do but wind her legs around his trim waist, hook them behind his back and slide her most sensitive spot over his impressive bulge?

Fee heard Clint's moan of appreciation and then his hand encircled the top of her leg, his fingers on the inside of her thigh, and Fee wished he had his hands on her naked flesh, that she could feel his clever mouth sucking her nipples, maybe even going lower.

His mouth, as she was coming to learn, was a weapon of mass temptation. Fee knew that if he asked, she'd eagerly follow him into his house and down the hallway to his bedroom, or whether he decided to stop. She would take whatever he'd give her, grateful to be the recipient of the profound pleasure he managed to pull to the surface.

They didn't need to talk, their bodies were better at communicating than they were. Fee felt Clint take a step and she felt the hard coolness of wood through her jeans, dimly realizing he'd planted her on the wide sill of a window.

He lifted his hands to hold her face, his thumbs caressing her cheekbones as he feathered kisses across her eyelids, down her temple. Fee closed her eyes, enjoying the moment of tenderness. Then Clint covered her right breast with his hand, and her nipple tightened, rising against the fabric of her sweater to press into his palm. Clint jerked his head back, looked at her with stormy eyes and muttered a quiet obscenity.

"Why aren't you pushing me away?" he hoarsely demanded.

"Why would I, since you kiss like a dream?" Fee responded, her voice just this side of breathy. Hearing his sharp intake of air, Fee decided to rock his boat a little more. "You are abrupt and annoying but, God, you know how to touch me."

Clint ran his knuckles up her ribcage and across her nipple. "Like this?" His fingers burrowed under her sweater and landed on her bare skin.

"Exactly like that," Fee murmured. Then Clint pulled down the lacy cup of her bra and pulled her nipple with his fingers. Fee couldn't help crying out.

Fee put her hand behind his head and shook her head. "No, don't stop! Do it again."

Clint's repeated the action and Fee arched her back, dropped her leg and banged her heel against the back of his lower thigh, just above his knee. Instead of bone and sinew, the heel of her boot bounced off metal hidden behind the fabric of his jeans.

Clint reacted like he'd been scorched. Leaping backward, he put a healthy amount of distance between them. He stared down at the floor as Fee tried to make sense of why he stopped.

The answer came to her on a quiet whisper: she'd kicked his prosthetic leg.

Well, okay then. No big deal…

"Come back here and kiss me, Rockwell," Fee suggested, wanting, no, needing his mouth on hers. She wasn't done with him, not yet.

Clint had frozen, his big arms folded across his chest, his face a blank mask. She didn't like the lack of emotion in his eyes, in his expression. She could handle pissed off and irritated, turned on and taciturn, but she didn't like this cyborg standing in front of her, acting like she was a fly he was getting ready to swat.

"I think it's time you went home," Clint said, in the blandest of bland tones. "You can take your gag money with you and start arrangements to pay me the twenty thousand we agreed upon."

They were back to this, really? "That number is just something you pulled out of your ass to piss me off, we both know it's stupidly excessive. As for leaving…"

Fee jumped down from the windowsill and walked up to Clint until her breasts brushed against his arms. She saw the flare of heat in his eyes and knew he was nowhere near as unaffected as he was pretending to be.

Good to know.

"I don't like mixed signals, Rockwell. You can't devour me one minute and ask me to leave the next."

"On my spread, I can do anything I damn well like," Clint muttered.

Fee cocked her head at his statement. "Now you're just sounding petulant. It's not a good look on you, Rockwell."

Clint rubbed his hand over his face. "Will you just go? Please?"

"No, not until we talk about why you jumped away from me like you were hit by a bolt of lightning."

Annoyance and frustration jumped into Clint's eyes and Fee didn't mind. She could deal with those emotions. She far preferred anger to his impassivity. "Let's break it down, shall we?" she continued.

"Let's not."

Fee ignored him. "You touched my boob and I banged the back of my heel against your prosthetic leg. Now, because I know that couldn't hurt you, there has to be another reason why you're overreacting."

Clint handed her a hard stare, his eyes reflecting confusion and more than a little fear. At what? What was the real problem here?

"You know I have a prosthetic leg."

Yes, she did. It was the least important thing she'd discovered about him. "I also know you are a billionaire, you were some sort of super soldier and now you are a semi-recluse, much to the dismay of the Royal residents, who've placed you somewhere between God and Friday-night football."

Finally, a hint of amusement touched his lips. "That's a huge exaggeration since I have little to do with them."

"Trust me, ten minutes dealing with your sarcasm and general orneriness would have them reevaluating your wonderfulness," Fee said, her tone tart. She slapped her hands on her hips. "But we're getting distracted from the point of this conversation."

Clint looked past her at something beyond her shoulder. "You're not going to let this go, are you?"

Damn straight. "No."

"I lost my left leg above my knee. When you kicked it, I realized I should stop this, now."

"Why?"

"To save both of us the embarrassment of you running out of here squealing when you see me, and it, fully exposed. It's not a pretty sight." Clint's smile was hard and his eyes glittered with pain-laced fury. "I don't need your sympathy or your pity. I just need sex."

Fee felt anger boil inside of her. She was angry at the people who had so obviously hurt him by making him feel less than, and angry at him for projecting those people's feelings onto her. Yes, she was a reality TV star but she wasn't shallow, dammit.

To make her point, Fee gathered a handful of Clint's T-shirt in her fist. She knew with a quick twist he could be free of her grasp, he did have a hundred pounds of muscle on her, but she was trying to make a point here.

"You just keep pissing me off, Rockwell. It's quite a talent," Fee murmured.

"Just get to the point, Seraphina. I've got work to do."

Fee pulled him over to the steps and pushed him down two of them so they were eye to eye, face to face. "That's better. Now, listen up because I'm only going to say this once…"

"Man, you're bossy."

"If I were a man, you'd call my behavior assertiveness," Fee quipped back.

"If you were a man, I would've had you in a headlock by now."

Fair point, Fee thought.

"And I certainly wouldn't have kissed you and we wouldn't be having this conversation," Clint continued.

Fee waved his words away. "I'm not going to get into an argument about semantics with you, Rockwell. Not right now anyway." Fee was surprised that Clint—a taciturn, will-only-use-one-word-when-three-are-needed man—was even arguing with her.

Fee placed her hands on either side of his face and rested her thumbs against his mouth. "Be. Quiet."

"Nothing makes me angrier than when someone who doesn't know me compares me to someone else," Fee told him, keeping her voice low but intense. "I'm lots of things—I have a hundred faults—but I am, one hundred percent, my own person. That means I make up my own mind and I get very pissed when people assume they know what's inside my head."

Clint narrowed his eyes at her and pulled his head out of her gentle grip. Fee held up her hand to silence him when he opened his mouth to speak. "Not done. I kissed you because, although you are annoying and frustrating, you're probably the best-looking guy I've stumbled across in a long, long time. You're tall, built, ripped and you kiss like you're in contention for an Olympic medal. You've got skills, Rockwell. I'm not going to deny that. And, yes, had you not behaved like a jerk—which seems to be something you specialize in—we might be naked right now. But you did, so we're not.

"I already knew you lost a leg, Rockwell, and I got the Royal diner version of how it happened. If I was turned off by your missing leg, I wouldn't have started something we couldn't finish. Again, I am lots of things, but I'm not a tease."

Fee handed him a hot look. "Fact, I want you. I wanted you the first time I saw you days ago when

I first visited Blackwood Hollow. I wanted you yesterday when I saw you barreling around the ring on your demon horse, looking sweaty and hot and, God, so alive."

His eyes heated and Fee forced herself to continue, to not go with her impulse and cover his mouth with hers. She needed to say this; she had to get her point across.

"I wanted you when you castigated me about my driving. I wanted you when I was showering, and in my dreams last night. When I heard about your having lost a leg, I felt, momentarily, sorry for you." She saw him jerk at the *S* word and shrugged it off. "I felt sorry for you because that's how nice people feel when they hear about something tragic happening to a good man. But that was quickly replaced with the 'how the hell does he ride so well with one leg?' thought."

"Seraphina—"

Since he was calling her by her full name, Fee knew she hadn't broken through yet. "I'm not done, Rockwell." Fee took a deep breath. "Judge me on my own words, Clint. My own actions. Don't judge me on someone else's stupidity. It's not right and it most certainly isn't fair."

Clint rubbed the back of his neck and stared down at the ground. It was a hell of a conversation to have after such a short acquaintance and a bruising kiss.

"And know this…" Fee concluded. "If I start something, I always finish it."

Clint raised his head, looking mystified and a little amused. "Where the hell did you come from, Seraphina Martins?"

"Martinez," she corrected. Fee stood up straight and just managed to drop a kiss on his jaw. "And I'm from everywhere. And nowhere."

She tapped her fingers lightly against the side of his jaw. "If we do this again, make sure you're prepared to let me in, to see you, to see all of you. Otherwise, don't bother."

A little bit of misery seeped into Clint's eyes. "I don't know if I can do that."

Fee rubbed her cheek against him, loving the feel of his scruff gently scratching her cheek. "That's your prerogative, Rockwell. If you can't, that's cool. But, for me, it's an all or nothing deal. You see me naked, I see you naked."

"You're whole, Fee, and I imagine you look glorious naked."

"Damn right I do." Fee dropped a small kiss onto his lips. "But beauty, as they say, is in the eye of the beholder, Clint."

She pulled back, spun around and picked up her tote bag from the floor. She looked down at the fake bundles of cash on the floor and picked up the real money and tucked the bills into the back pocket of her jeans. She tossed Clint a look over her shoulder.

"Also, while you are deciding whether you want to sleep with me or not, how about you stop messing with me about how much the repairs are going to cost and give me a figure that's in the ballpark of reasonable?"

"Of course I *want* to sleep with you, Fee," Clint said.

Fee sent him a small smile. "But not enough, Clint, not just yet."

And that was okay, she'd allow him a little time to get there. Men always needed a little extra time to get with the program.

Her program was simple—rope a cowboy, ride him hard and get him out of her system.

Really, this shouldn't be so hard.

Three

Whoever had the bright idea that the New York socialites should learn something about ranching should be shot, Clint decided. And the person who decided Clint should oversee the process should be tortured, then shot.

Back at Blackwood Hollow, Clint fought to hide his impatience as he stood outside a stall in the bigger of the two stable blocks and listened to Miranda DuPree-Blackwood and her Italian bombshell colleague bitch about the smell, the dirty hay and the smell of horse.

Well, it was a stable, and to be fair, only the brunette was bitching. Miranda just had a determined look on her face as she pitched hay into a barrow while the brunette—Rachel, Rafel... *Rafaela—*

examined her nails. Clint turned around to glare at the director who was making notes on her clipboard, her iPad tucked under her arm.

Damn you, Buck, for complicating the hell out of your death.

"You do realize we have work to do and we can't hang around here all day waiting for these—" he bit back the word he really wanted to say "—*ladies* to get out of our way?" Clint demanded. He had his own ranch to look after once everything was running smoothly at Blackwood Hollow. Yet again, he cursed the day he'd agreed to keep an eye on the place after Buck got sick. He should have stuck to his role as the town hermit and said no, but while his grandfather's old friend was irascible and hard-assed, he'd had, under his prickly exterior, a heart of gold few people got to see. Buck had also kept an eye on Rockwell Ranch after Gramps died, so Clint owed him.

And he always, always, paid off his debts.

"Miranda owns this place, there's an inheritance saga, a family feud and, on top of that, the *Secret Lives* stars know nothing about ranching. I know this is frustrating but it will make fantastic TV."

Great, because that was what he cared about, making fantastic TV. He had cows to feed, fence stays to cut for repair work and he wanted to put a new wood stove in the calving barn so the calves born in late winter had a better chance of survival.

Thank God the oil side of his business was leased and the day-to-day issues associated with that business weren't his problem.

Miranda, with hay in her hair, poked her head out from the stall. "You don't need to be here, Clint. I'm sure Gabe can show us the ropes."

Gabe, Buck's longest employee, gave him a *don't leave me alone with them* look. While Miranda had inherited Blackwood Hollow and everything else from Buck, she knew diddly-squat about ranching and she couldn't afford to annoy the staff, especially Gabe.

Gabe knew the ranch inside out and Miranda, whether she knew it or not, needed him. And the man looked frustrated and irritated and was, obviously, itching to leave.

Clint sighed. "Gabe, you carry on with the rest of your work. I'll look after this lot."

Gratitude flashed in the older man's eyes and he didn't bother to argue, he just hightailed it out of the barn as fast as he could. Clint fought the urge to run after him.

He turned back to the director, who held a clipboard to her chest. "How much more do you need?"

"Well, I thought we could film Rafaela learning to saddle a horse and taking her first riding lesson, Miranda collecting eggs from the chicken run and Lulu filling the horse nets with food."

Yeah, because that's what ranching was really about. Collecting eggs and feeding horses. What about counting the livestock, branding, checking for pregnancies, land management? Worrying about too little rain, too much rain, stock theft, beef prices, whether they had enough feed to see them through the winter after a very dry summer?

"I need to film Seraphina doing something farmy, too."

Clint held back his snort. *Farmy?* God help him.

"I can assign hands to show the ladies the ropes for the tasks you had in mind, and I can show Fee how we transport bales of hay to the pastures so the cattle have enough to eat during these winter months," Clint suggested.

"Someone mention my name?"

Clint turned and his heart kicked up when he heard her chirpy voice. He slowly turned around and he had to smile at the sight of Fee in cowgirl mode again. Her long hair was in two thick braids hanging down over her flannel shirt, which was worn over an old pair of jeans. She wore rain boots printed with— Clint leaned forward and squinted at her feet—ducks wearing rain boots.

She had a streak of dirt across her cheek and she looked like she'd actually been doing some work instead of just playing at it.

"Lu and I are done in this stall. What's next?" Fee asked, rubbing her hands on the seat of her pants.

Clint used his height to peek over the stable door and was impressed by the full water trough and clean floor covered by fresh straw.

And they hadn't taken forever to do it.

The director consulted her clipboard. "Why don't you go with Clint and Jimmy? He can film you taking something somewhere."

Clint summoned the little patience he had left. "Hay bales to the feed stations in the pastures," Clint told her.

"Cool. How do we get the hay out there? Do we put it in wheelbarrows?"

Clint had to smile. "Since the bales are over a ton each, that would be difficult. We use a lifter…" He closed his eyes at the thought of Fee operating the lifter with its two massive forks. With her lead foot, who knew what damage she'd do?

"Yay, I get to drive." Fee bounced on her toes, looking excited.

Worst idea ever, Clint decided, as Fee bounded for the door. Clint turned to the director. "I hope your insurance and liabilities policies are up to date since Fee is a maniac behind the wheel."

"Don't break anything, Fee!" Miranda shouted from the inside the stable, obviously listening to their conversation.

"Yeah, Fee, don't break anything," Lulu said, coming to stand in the doorway of the stall. She smiled at Fee and then her expression changed and her eyes cooled. Clint looked over his shoulder to see Kace LeBlanc, standing by the sliding door at the entrance of the stable block, a dark brown Stetson throwing shadows across his face.

LeBlanc seemed to be everywhere the socialites were. Clint couldn't decide if he was taking his job as Buck's lawyer to heart by hovering around Miranda, or if his true motive was because the NYC tourists were all stunningly attractive.

But Kace only seemed to have eyes for Lulu.

Clint pulled his eyes back to Fee, who stood with her hand on her heart, her eyes full of mischief. A cameraman stood behind him, the camera pointed in Fee's direction. Clint stood aside so he wasn't in the shot. "I am truly saddened by your lack of faith in me, Miranda."

"I came by it naturally," Miranda said as she walked out of the stable, trailed by another cameraman and Rafaela who, judging by her still spotless clothes, hadn't lifted a finger to help muck out the stall.

"You did put your hand into Abby's wedding cake, and you did nearly set the kitchen on fire when we were filming in the Hamptons because you left oil on the stove. You did fall off a bar in Cancun," Miranda pointed out. "You really should stop dancing on bars."

Fee pulled a face. "That was Lulu."

"We both fell off the bar in Dublin," Lulu corrected her. "You fell off the bar in Cancun because you were flirting with the bartender and weren't looking where you were going."

Fee shook her head and her braids bounced off her shoulders. "I dispute that." She looked around and frowned. "Where's Zooey?"

"Present."

Clint turned at the faint voice drifting over to them and he saw another woman standing at the entrance to the stable, a cowboy hat tipped over her eyes, her booted foot resting against the barn wall behind her.

Clint heard Fee's huge sigh and watched as she walked over to her friend and pushed up her hat. The cameras would pick up what he saw: a pale blonde with blue-ringed eyes, looking like she was dealing with the hangover from hell.

"Aw, honey," Fee crooned, stroking her arm from shoulder to elbow. "You look like crap, Zo."

"Feel like crap. Too many shooters with too many cowboys," Zooey replied.

That would do it.

The director turned to Clint. "I need something for Zooey to do. I have to film her doing something, preferably sitting down."

What was he, a friggin' consultant? "Get her to clean some tack." He walked up to where Fee was standing and put his hand on her back. When she looked at him with those delicious brown eyes, his heart spluttered.

Stupid thing.

"I really need to get going. You coming or not?"

"Always so gracious," Fee murmured. She looked back at the director and flashed a smile. "I'm going to feed the cows."

"Excellent. Take Jimmy with you."

Clint looked at the tall, lanky man holding a camera to his shoulder and rolled his eyes. Fabulous.

No, super fabulous.

Because, how exactly was he supposed to kiss the hell out of her when he had an audience?

* * *

Fee parked the lifter where she'd found it and slapped her hands on the steering wheel, immensely pleased with herself. She'd thought she'd be driving a tractor but could see why this machine was so effective. She shoved the prongs of the lifter into a massive bale of hay, lifted it up and transported it to a feeding trough in a nearby pasture. She'd cut the twine off the bale—using Clint's multi-tool—and returned the lifter to its parking spot, all without injuring herself, Clint, Jimmy or the machine itself.

Nothing to this ranching stuff!

Jimmy dropped his camera and held it to his side. "I'm going to take off, Fee. Do you want to walk with me back to the barn?"

Fee glanced at Clint, who'd hopped off the lifter. "No, I'll catch up with you." She glanced at her watch. "Where are we filming this afternoon?"

"We've got the afternoon off," Jimmy reminded her.

"Excellent." She glanced at Clint who was staring down at his phone, his expression intense. "Tell Lu and the rest that I'll see them when I see them."

"Cool."

When he was out of earshot, Fee hopped down from her seat and walked around the back of the machine to where Clint stood, still looking troubled. "Problem?"

"I was just checking the weather app—it's an occupational hazard." Clint looked a little distracted. "There's a forecast for high winds."

"Winds are a problem?"

"They can be," Clint replied. "We experienced a drought this past summer, and the grass and lands are dry. We typically start to worry about fires later in the season but even now, because it's so dry, one spark can set off a hell of a blaze."

Fee looked around, saw the brown grass and the cattle in the pastures and shuddered. "That wouldn't be good."

Clint handed her one of his almost smiles. "It wouldn't." He gestured to the lifter. "You did well. Now, you have to do that another fifteen times today to feed all the livestock in the paddocks closest to the house. And we haven't even started getting feed to the livestock in the far pastures."

Fee looked aghast. "How many more times?"

Clint's slow smile caused her stomach to flip over. "Relax, I'm not going to ask you to do it. Gabe and the hands will finish up."

"Thank God," Fee said, putting her hands on her lower back and stretching. "That seat is not good for my back."

She noticed his eyes went to her breasts, and she didn't mind. In fact, she loved the flash of desire in his eyes. "Back problems?" he asked, his voice lower and huskier than before.

"Yeah. A gate fell on me when I was a kid and I've struggled with back issues ever since. Especially when I do something different and, trust me, mucking out stalls and hopping on and off machinery is very different from my normal exercise routine."

Clint walked behind her and placed his hands on her waist, his thumbs digging into two spots in her lower back. Fee groaned as sweet pain flooded her system. God, his fingers felt so good.

He moved his hands up, holding her rib cage, thumbs pushing into another set of knots and she moaned again.

"You're as tight as a drum," Clint murmured, his breath warm against her ear. She shivered, wanting to turn around and slap her mouth against his.

Hellfire, she wanted him.

Without turning around, she lifted his big hands over her breasts, arching her back to push her nipples into his broad palms. "I still want you."

Clint's thumbs swiped over her, eliciting a groan of pleasure. "Are you sure?"

Fee whipped around, instantly annoyed. "What do you need me to do, take out an ad in your local newspaper?"

Clint's mouth twitched. "Point taken." She saw him hesitate and she waited for his next excuse. Yeah, she understood his reluctance to get naked, but unless he was resigned to a celibate lifestyle, he was going to have to get over it.

Clint pulled her back into his chest, the ridge of his erection pushing into her lower back. "Come home with me."

Finally. Fee allowed her lips to curve upward. "An excellent plan. We'll take my car—it's parked out front."

"I've got a better idea."

Fee stiffened. "Not by horse, please. Firstly, it will take too long since I don't ride and also my back is already killing me.'

"Not by horseback, not today anyway," Clint told her, taking her hand and leading her to the back of the barn and then behind the stables to where a muddy dirt bike was parked.

Clint slung his leg over the seat and tipped his head. "Climb on, peanut."

Fee placed her hand on his shoulder, swung her leg over and felt herself sliding down the seat into Clint's back, her breasts pushed against his flannel shirt. When she wrapped her arms around his waist, he rested his big hand on her thigh and squeezed. "You okay?"

Fee wiggled and she smiled when Clint tensed. Yep, she was pretty sure that if she dropped her hand and allowed it to fall lower, she'd find something long and hard and ready to play. "I'm good. You?"

"My jeans are suddenly about two sizes too small," Clint admitted.

Before she could reply, he gunned the accelerator and Fee squealed as they took off. She tightened her hold on him, instinctively realizing she had to move as he did, trusting him to keep them upright.

After a few minutes, she knew Clint was as good on a bike as he was on a horse and she relaxed, spreading her fingers across his stomach, allowing one hand to drift up his chest. Instead of taking the main road, Clint cut across the ranch, using trails, skirting trees and rocks.

When they hit an open piece of land, Clint lifted one hand to cover hers with his, holding it against his heart.

It was such a small gesture but, in that instant, she felt utterly connected to this man, and to the land he knew so well.

And seemed to love as much.

They passed through a gate and Clint informed her she was now on Rockwell land, pointing out the oil derricks in the distance.

"The Rockwell wealth was built on oil and ranching," Clint told her, above the noise of the engine and the whistling wind.

"Is your father not involved in the ranch at all?"

Clint's grip on her fingers tightened. "He died when I was five. My folks separated when I was a baby and my dad, initially, had custody. When he died, I moved to Dallas with my mom but I spent every holiday here at the ranch with my grandfather. My grandfather left the ranch to me when he died."

They were getting personal and that wasn't supposed to happen. She didn't do permanent and he didn't seem to do people, so this was a one-off thing.

"So, all this land is yours?"

"Yep." Clint slowed down to allow a cow to cross the trail they were riding and sent her a mischievous look over his shoulder. "I also own a ranch close to Austin."

She loved his bad-boy look, his charming half smile, his closeness. Fee was surprised her ovaries hadn't exploded yet. "Good thing I'm only interested in your body, not your acreage," Fee lightly replied.

"Good thing," Clint quipped as he swung the bike off one trail and onto another. Within a few minutes Fee caught glimpses of his sprawling house and she swallowed a burst of panic. What was she doing, literally riding off with a cowboy? Despite her party-hearty reputation, she didn't do one-night, or afternoon, stands; she never hopped into bed with strangers.

But there was something about Clint, something that called to her. Maybe it was the hint of vulnerability she'd heard in his voice or the sadness and loneliness she'd seen in his eyes.

She wanted him, sure, but she also wanted to make him feel a little treasured, a little cherished, even if they were only destined to spend a few hours together. Because she suspected it had been a long time, if ever, since Clint was cherished, treasured.

He probably wouldn't recognize either one if it bit him on the butt.

Clint skirted his barns and the paddock, beautiful horses with patterned coats raising their heads at the sound of the bike. He sped toward the imposing front of the house with its wrap-around veranda and stately front door.

Fee heard his low curse and saw a white SUV parked next to a quad bike and a brand-new pickup with a Rockwell Ranch logo on the door.

He parked his bike next to the SUV, hopped off and scowled. "Is today the twentieth?"

"All day," Fee answered, climbing off the bike.

Clint ran his hand through his dark blond, wind-blown hair. "My physiotherapist is here. I forgot she was coming today."

Ah. So, no afternoon sex then. Damn.

"You're still having physio?" Fee asked as she followed him up the stairs and through the big wooden door into a spacious hallway.

"Only once a month now. Sam comes to check up on my progress and to make sure I am not over-doing it."

"In what way?" Fee asked, looking into the luxurious great room with floor-to-ceiling windows, massive, comfortable-looking couches and a huge fireplace. Bright art adorned the walls and Fee was grateful she couldn't see any dead animal heads mounted on the walls.

She wasn't a fan of taxidermy in any shape or form.

"She's both a physio and a trainer, so she was able to get me back in shape after too long lying around, recuperating. Sam also helped me with my various prosthetics, learning how to use them, to program them."

He frowned slightly, looking a little embarrassed. "I don't know what I would've done without her these past two years so, as much as I want to whip you off to bed, I'm going to have to take a rain check, just for an hour or two."

Fee wondered what she was expected to do while

she waited for him. Or if she should wait for him at all. Maybe this wasn't such a good idea.

She glanced at the front door. "Maybe I should go. But I'd have to borrow a vehicle from you."

Clint grinned and her heart sighed. "You're a maniac behind the wheel, Martinez, so that's not going to happen." Clint took her hand in his and squeezed. "Don't run off, Fee. Please?"

Before she could answer him, Clint tugged her down the long, cool hallway. Where were they going? Surely he wasn't intending to stuff her into his bedroom and expecting her to wait for him like a good little girl?

"Maybe we should table this for another day."

"Nope." Clint stopped in front of a half-open door, and he closed his eyes. "You might as well come in, meet Sam, see me. After Sam's tortured me, you can then decide if you want to stay or go."

Fee immediately knew what he was saying. If she watched his physio, she'd see him wearing his prosthetic, a prelude to seeing him naked, which was his most vulnerable state. He was giving her, and him, a gentler way to back out if she changed her mind.

Which he clearly kept expecting her to do. But he didn't know she was stubborn, and once she set her mind on something, she generally never backed down.

And, she knew with every fiber of her being, no matter how bad his leg looked, she would still want him.

Because she wasn't only attracted to his fallen

angel face and his wide chest and big arms, flat stomach and thick legs, she was attracted to his soul, to his determination, to his unwillingness to stop doing what he wanted to do because he was missing a limb.

He rode horses like a crazy person, worked his ranch, rode his dirt bike. He wasn't sitting in a darkened room refusing to face life—people, maybe, but not life—and she admired his drive and persistence.

So many people would just throw their hands in the air and embrace being a victim of life's unfairly dealt cards.

Fee wouldn't change her mind about sleeping with him and the only way to prove her intention was to *not* change her mind.

She gestured to the door and bumped his shoulder with hers. "Rockwell, we're only going to get to the fun stuff if you hop to it."

The words flew out of her mouth and she only realized what she'd said when they hovered in the suddenly awkward silence between them. Fee glanced at Clint, hoping he didn't think she was mocking his disability, and she sighed in relief when she saw a flash of amusement in his eyes.

He might've lost half his leg but he hadn't, entirely, lost his ability to smile.

Thank God because she seldom thought before she spoke and she was known to be occasionally inappropriate. And irreverent.

But, hopefully, never cruel.

Four

Clint saw Sam out, and when he returned, he found Fee curled up in the easy chair in the corner of his expensive home gym, one leg dangling over an arm. Earlier he'd changed from jeans into exercise shorts and a tank for his training session with Sam, and he was conscious of his matted hair and damp chest but mostly of his matte black prosthetic.

Do or die time.

Clint pushed down the panic threatening to close his chest. Fee was one of the few women he'd allowed to see the stump tucked into his prosthetic for a long, long time. Would she bolt? She kept saying she wouldn't, but he'd learned to trust what people did, not what they said. Time for the truth, he thought as he stood in front of her, his arms folded over his chest. She'd either handle it or she wouldn't; he wouldn't allow himself to care either way.

He'd stopped caring about his mom's opinion—*I like pretty and I like perfect*—and he shouldn't care about Fee's since she was leaving in a few weeks to go back east, so why was his heart in his mouth? Why was his stomach twisted like a pretzel?

He was so pathetic, because, dammit, when he saw female appreciation in her eyes, when she looked at him like she wanted to devour him whole, he felt like the man he used to be.

He felt strong and capable and powerful and whole… He wasn't, but she made him feel that way.

Fee swung her legs off the chair and leaned forward, examining his prosthetic. It was one of the most advanced devices on the planet and he had a full range of movement; it was just a marvel of modern technology.

But, funny thing, he'd still prefer his old leg back.

Fee rested her fingers on what should've been his knee, allowing her fingers to drift up to the suction cup. "Is it sore?"

"No. Not anymore," he answered. "It's an ugly wound but not sore."

"Phantom pains?"

Someone had done their research. He was both pleased and terrified. "Yeah, I get those but less often than I did. They are pretty annoying."

"Why do I suspect that's your way of saying they hurt like a bitch but that you would rather die than admit it?"

She was spot on. They *did* hurt like a bitch but he wasn't one for whining. Fee kept her hand on him and looked up through long, thick lashes. "I went online and read up on what you did to save your teammates, Clint. You were amazing, so focused and so brave."

There was nothing amazing about it. He'd done what he had to do to save his friends; he would not let them die in a tangle of metal in a foreign country. "Any of them would've done the same."

"Maybe, maybe not. But you were the one who did and, I know this sounds weird, considering we barely know each other but—" Fee hesitated and he saw the glint of tears in her eyes. Or a crapload of emotion. Suddenly he really wanted to know what she was about to say…no, he *needed* to know.

"But?"

Fee dropped her hand and looked at the floor, shaking her head. He cupped her jaw and tipped her face up. "What, Fee?"

She looked embarrassed. "I was just going to say I'm proud of you but that sounds weird because, you know, we don't know each other." She waved her hand in front of her eyes as if to dry the moisture. "Anyway, I'm sure your family is very proud of you."

He almost laughed at her statement. Proud? Definitely not.

He was good PR—Mila frequently mentioned her wounded war hero, Purple Heart–recipient son on her prime time news slot—but his mom hadn't want to deal with the reality of having a son who'd needed numerous operations, spent months in the hospital and who had to undergo rigorous rehabilitation to get back on one foot. Even before he was injured, he'd always been too much trouble for her, distracting her from what was important, which was making sure she was the most visible, most powerful, journalist in Dallas.

Fee was the first person he'd allowed to broach the subject, to talk about the past. And being Fee, she just looked him straight in the eye and spoke with pity and sentimentality.

"Thank you," he said, his voice husky. He felt her hand drift onto his thigh, above his suction cup, her fingers resting lightly on his scarred skin.

"Let me see you, Clint. All of you."

It was such a big step…she was asking him to strip down, to show his most vulnerable self. With his prosthetic removed, he either needed to sit down or use his crutches, neither of which screamed rampant sex god. He would be vulnerable…

He reminded himself that she was half his size and he was trained; she couldn't hurt him if she tried. He was still a highly trained army ranger and she wasn't dangerous, not to his safety anyway. His heart maybe, but he wasn't going there…

What was the worst she could do? Laugh? Run away? Well, that had happened before and he'd survived. He'd survived his mom's lack of interest and, after losing his friends and his limb, knew he could survive anything.

But, still…

I like pretty and I like perfect...

Clint cursed, not sure if he could do this. He wasn't ready.

He didn't know if he'd ever be.

"It's okay, Clint, really," Fee said, standing up and wrapping her arms around his waist she placed her forehead on his sternum and he looked down at her mass of black curls. "I'm really pushy—it's one of my worst traits."

Clint laid his hand on her head. "I'm not pushable."

"I know," Fee said, looking up at him. "You're the most stubborn man I've ever met."

"Pot calling the kettle black, Fee?"

Fee smiled at him and his heart cracked, just a little. He'd patch it up later, before the chasm widened and he started to think of this woman in terms of tomorrow and more.

He just wanted a night, maybe a few nights, and then he would say goodbye, wave her on her way. They had today, maybe tomorrow, and he didn't intend to waste any time. But right now, he wanted to lay hands on this woman, and not in the way she thought he would.

Giving her a massage would give him some time to think, to gather his courage to let her see him, to take a chance.

"Why don't you lie on the massage table, face down?" Clint suggested.

Fee looked at the massage table in the corner of the gym, the one where Sam had worked on him earlier. "Why?"

"Trust me," Clint said, taking her hand and leading her across the room. Fee sat on the edge of the bed and he yanked off her rain boots—taking a moment to inspect the ducks. Shaking his head, he tossed them to one side and reached for the button on the band of her jeans.

Fee stopped him by frowning, placing her hand on his. He looked down and grimaced. "Sorry, I have heard about foreplay, I promise—but that's not what this is. I just wanted to loosen your pants a bit so I can massage your lower back."

"You're going to give me a massage?" Fee asked, her eyes round with surprise.

"Well, yeah." Why else did she think she was on this table? He was out of practice but he hadn't forgotten everything he knew about women. Their first time deserved a bed, not a hard table in a gym. "I've seen you grimace a few times and you keep stretching as if you are cramping."

"You really have to observe less and explain more, Rockwell," Fee said, flipping onto her stomach and pushing her jeans down to her hips. Clint's mouth dropped open when she lifted her torso and whipped off her shirt, baring the crisscross straps of her purple bra to his very appreciative gaze.

Acres of creamy skin, three freckles just below her left shoulder blade, the bumps of her spine. Clint wanted to kiss the hollow of her back, the two small dimples he could see at the top of her butt, and he would, sometime this afternoon.

But, for now, he wanted her loose and liquid. Not

wanting to ruin her beautiful bra, he asked her if he could unhook it and when she nodded, he separated the hooks and eyes, allowing the purple fabric to bunch on the bed at her sides. He picked up her hair, draped it over her shoulder and lifted a few loose tendrils off her elegant neck.

He had no idea how he was going to massage her without getting distracted. Clint poured some massage oil into his hands, rubbed them together and took a deep breath as he stroked the oil onto her skin. He sucked in a hot, aroused, confused breath as he dug his fingers into her muscles. He'd had women before, lots of them and he'd never felt this turned on, this on edge.

This was life changing, important, breath stealing…

And she shouldn't be. He wouldn't let her be.

He had to stop giving her more importance in his life than she had. This was about sex, about a moment in time, about physical release.

Stop thinking, Rockwell, your head is going to explode. And that wasn't the explosion he was most looking forward to. That one would happen three feet lower…

Fifteen minutes later and he was nearly done. Clint dug his fingers into a knot beneath Fee's shoulders and heard her low groan, felt her shudder. He couldn't wait any longer, he needed her, here, now…

He couldn't deny himself any longer…

"Roll over, Seraphina," he commanded and she did, holding her sexy bra to her breasts as she sat up. He cocked an eyebrow, amused by her reticence. She was loud and bold—he hadn't expected shyness. He hooked a finger under a cup of her bra and gently tugged. Fee sucked her bottom lip into her mouth and allowed the fabric to fall into her lap. Clint felt the punch to his heart, another to his stomach as she leaned back on her hands, allowing him to look...

And look.

She was cream and Cointreau and he knew she'd taste as good as she looked. "You are the most beautiful woman I have ever seen."

The flash of surprise in her eyes told him too few lovers had mentioned her beauty. He dragged his finger across her collarbone, down the slope of her breast and over her puckered nipple. *So responsive*, he thought. He placed his hands on her breasts, tested their weight, enjoying their fullness. Man, she was hot and yeah, he wanted her.

But not here...

Clint banded his arm around her waist and pulled her so that she sat on the edge of the massage bed and he stepped into the space between her legs. "Let's take this to the bedroom. Hook your legs around my waist."

"Okay but...first..." Fee scooted closer, draped her arms around his neck and Clint sucked in his breath when she slid her mouth across his. Her tongue traced his bottom lip and all his good intentions to take this slowly evaporated.

He needed her...now.

Clint took control of the kiss, plundering her mouth as if this were the last time he'd kiss a woman, the last time he'd have this experience. Instead of pulling back, Fee met him stroke for stroke, twisting her tongue around his and pushing her bare breasts into his chest. Frustrated at the lack of skin-on-skin contact, Clint pulled his tank over his head and then her hands were on his ribcage, sliding up and over his chest, moving around to his back. She pushed her hand under the band of his exercise shorts, growling her frustration.

"I need you, now," Fee muttered and Clint's last shred of control was obliterated.

This was going to happen in his gym, on a Tuesday afternoon a week before Christmas. Best present ever.

Clint dropped his hands to her jeans and this time she didn't stop him when he slid the zipper all the way down, pushing the opening apart so he could slide his hands inside. He sucked a nipple into his mouth and laved it while working her jeans down her hips. Fee lifted one butt cheek to help him, then the other and soon her jeans and panties were on the floor, and Fee wasted no time in making sure his exercise shorts and boxer briefs joined the pile of clothing.

He stood naked before her and, not wanting to give her time to think or pull back, reached for her, needing passion to take over, to take them away.

But Fee placed a hand on his heart, those exquisite eyes connecting with his. "Let me see you, Clint. I need to see you."

Clint knew he could distract her with a quick,

hard kiss but Fee's request was powerful, sweet and not easy to deny. Tensing, he watched her face as he stepped back, feeling her eyes on his chest, his groin area and finally his leg. A part of him was relieved that he was standing, that he couldn't take off his prosthetic.

He wasn't quite ready...

"You are so beautiful, so powerful," Fee murmured, her finger running over the biceps in his left arm. "You're so ripped, so muscular but not too much. Your body is... God, spectacular."

He couldn't remember when he'd last blushed but knew he was damn close to it now. "You need your eyes tested, Martinez."

Her eyes collided with his and she shook her head. "Don't do that, okay? Don't minimize how far you've come, how hard you've worked. You took a hit, one direct to your leg, and you not only survived, you goddamn conquered. I'm in awe of you, Clint. What's happening with us might only be a ships-passing-in-the-night thing but I can still appreciate your determination, your persistence."

He felt ten feet tall, like he could take on the world. To have such a woman—gorgeous, smart and mouthy—talk this way about him, lust and admiration and appreciation in her eyes, filled his soul with something that might be happiness.

Happiness...not an emotion he was terribly familiar with. And it scared him. He didn't want to get a taste of it and have to live without it. It was better to strive for contentment, for comfort and satisfaction.

And talking about satisfaction…

"You're pretty spectacular yourself," Clint said. "Can we please stop talking now?"

Fee's eye roll was accompanied by a smile. "I like to talk, Rockwell, get used to it."

"I noticed." Clint held her face in her hands. "Now, shut up and kiss me."

"I can do that."

Still standing in front of her, Clint covered her mouth with his, pulling her legs around his waist so skin met skin, breast to chest, the V of her legs pressed into his cock. This…man.

Touching Fee was what he never knew he needed.

Clint wrenched his mouth off hers, his attention on the warmth and moisture heating his cock. "I need you, Fee. I need to be inside you but I need to protect you. And the condoms are in my bedroom."

Fee just hooked one ankle behind the other and pressed her heels into his back. "I'm on the pill and I'm clean. If you can say the same, let's not move."

Could he risk it? Should he? He knew he was clean but he never, ever placed so much control in someone else's hands. But it would also take a momentous effort to disengage, to walk away. Just this once, this one time, he would take a chance.

Clint kissed her again, his hand sliding between their bodies to test her readiness and when she bucked into his fingers, moaned in his ear, he pushed into her, keeping his thumb on her clit.

Fee's moans were incomprehensible, a mixture of English and Spanish and girl-on-the-edge groans.

She scooted even closer to him and dug her finger-nails into his butt.

Clint kissed her with a ferocity he took to a fire-fight and buried himself to the hilt, his eyes crossing at the wonder of being in her, holding her, kissing her...

She was falling apart in his arms and he loved it.

Fee's nails dug deeper, her hips lifted and he felt her inner channel clench, demanding his response. She was close, and he couldn't wait. Needing her to come, he surged into her, placing his hands under her butt to tilt her up and she gasped and...

Yeah, gushed. On him, through him, around him.

Clint felt the pressure build in his balls, at the base of his spine, and he plunged deeper into her, needing more, needing everything.

Fee released an *oh-oh-oh* in his ear, and he came with all the force of a missile strike. Earth was de-stroyed, he was the conqueror...

Clint buried his face in Fee's sweet-smelling neck, the thought occurring that, by not being able to re-sist her, he might be the one who was vanquished, the one who was obliterated.

And right now, at this moment, he was okay with defeat.

Five

Unlike her costars who worked with personal trainers in air-conditioned gyms, Fee preferred running to keep herself in shape. So, after a meeting with the producer, director and the rest of the cast, she strapped her phone to her arm, pushed wireless buds into her ears and hit the road.

Running through Royal was a pleasure. It was a pretty town and the traffic was light at eight thirty on a Monday morning. Christmas, thank God, was over and she'd spent the holiday with her parents in Florida. Her visit had been short, less than thirty-six hours, and because her parents left for a cruise the day after Christmas, she didn't have to make excuses to return to Royal.

Her costars were also back in town and it was

business as usual. The feud between the Blackwood siblings and Miranda raged on unabated, Buck's illegitimate son had yet to be found—Miranda had told her about Buck's request for him to be found and asked she not repeat that news to anyone, not even Lulu (and she hadn't)—and the director of *Secret Lives* was milking the tension for all it was worth.

And, bonus, they didn't have to write the storyline…

Trying to relax, Fee looked at the Christmas decorations still gracing the homes and lawns of Royal residents. Their yards were well tended, the Christmas decorations were picture-postcard. It was obvious the Royal residents were proud of their homes and their town. She could see why. It really did seem like the perfect place for someone looking to settle down and build not just a life but a legacy for generations to come. The sheer permanence of everything—the post office that had stood for more than a century, the diner that had been on Main Street for decades—continued to surprise her.

Fee knew nothing was permanent—her parents had taught her that lesson—and for her, putting faith in a relationship, in a town, in a friend, was asking for trouble.

She didn't belong anywhere, not even in New York City. Manhattan was just a place to temporarily lay her head and when *Secret Lives* ended—and she was a realist, it would end—she would find another city, another place to live while she wrote the next chapter of her life.

That could be in Barcelona or Bogota, Riyadh or...Royal.

Fee stopped abruptly, her expensive running shoes scraping the pavement. Where on earth had that thought come from? Yes, Royal was a pretty town but it was too small, too farmy for her. She wasn't a small-town girl, she needed the energy of the city, to be able to browse specialist bookstores, visit art galleries and museums, go to cocktail parties and to the ballet.

But when last did you go clubbing, or to an art gallery? she asked herself. *When last did you go to a party that wasn't work related? You claim to love the city but you don't avail yourself of what it offers...*

Fee started jogging again, wondering why she was so at odds with herself. She'd been feeling this way since before Christmas, since leaving Clint Rockwell's bed.

They had, after making very good use of his massage table, moved to his room where they had spent the rest of the afternoon, and a good part of the evening, in a haze of orgasmic pleasure. She, obviously, noticed that he kept his prosthetic on throughout and she hadn't asked him to remove it.

His leg, his choice.

At ten, she'd dressed and Clint had, without argument, driven her back to her hotel. They'd parted with no promises to get in touch, skipping the obligatory *I'll call you*s. Through silent but mutual agreement, they both knew one night was all they could have, was all either of them could cope with.

She because Clint was too compelling for comfort, he because…who knew?

It didn't matter. They'd slept together, it was fun and it was over. It was all good…

And a little confusing because, since that night, rogue, stupid thoughts kept jumping into her brain, causing her to falter, to question her freewheeling life. What was up with that?

Fee stopped at an intersection, looked both ways and noticed a large construction site down the road, next to a smaller building with an old fire engine parked outside. The new building looked mostly finished but what caught and held her attention was the tall figure dressed in dark blue chinos and a pale blue button-down shirt under a gray pullover. Her heart kicked up and started to thump erratically.

Clint was dressed up, looking good and spending the morning in Royal. The town's most reclusive citizen had graced the town with his presence. Why?

You're just curious, Fee told herself. *You are not excited to see him. You are not desperate to hear his deep voice, to see whether his hazel eyes are green, gold or gray today. He's just a guy you had carnal relations with…*

And Shakespeare was just a writer, and Mandela was just another activist.

Annoyed with herself, Fee debated whether to run past the fire station. If she went left instead of right, it would add another three miles to her run and she'd already run three. Running past the fire station was the shorter route and she couldn't afford to take the extra time.

She had a full schedule today. They were filming at Blackwood Hollow and she and Lulu were scheduled to do a scene where they'd discuss what they intended to wear to the Texas Cattleman's Club New Year's Eve ball. Miranda had persuaded Nigel Townsend, owner of the production company responsible for *Secret Lives of NYC Ex-Wives*, to sponsor the event, to say thank you to the good residents of Royal for allowing them to film their town and have cameras and microphones shoved in their faces.

Fee had a schedule and she was, despite what the world thought, a professional. She hated being late so she'd have to run past Clint and the men he was talking to.

It had nothing to do with the fact she really, really, desperately wanted to speak to the sexy cowboy again.

Annoyed with herself, Fee ran down the road, pretending not to have noticed Rockwell. But she knew the exact moment when he noticed her. She felt her skin prickle, then flush with heat.

What if he ignores me? What if he pretends he hasn't seen me?

"Hey, peanut."

Although she wasn't crazy about the nickname, she was grateful to hear his voice seeping past the buds in her ears. Stopping, she turned around slowly and pulled them from ears. Crossing the road, she walked up to the construction fence and brushed a curl off her cheek. "Hey."

Oh, scintillating opening line, Seraphina. Use your words, girl.

Clint's eyes traveled up her body, taking in her skin-tight exercise pants and sleeveless crop top. Her eyes connected with his and she saw passion flicker gold in all that green. Gesturing at the suits with him, Clint quickly introduced his companions, who were architects from Dallas.

"I think we're done here, Clint," the oldest of the trio said, holding out his hand for Clint to shake.

"Thanks. And I can expect the building to be fit for occupation by the middle of January?" Clint asked.

"Absolutely. If not sooner."

As they said their goodbyes, Fee walked down the fence until she found a gate and went inside the construction site, staying close to the perimeter so she wouldn't be in the way of any of the busy crew.

She placed her hands on her hips and when Clint joined her, she pulled her eyes off the building to his face. "So, this project has to be fairly important to drag you off your ranch—" she gestured to his elegant clothes "—and into a nice outfit."

Clint jammed his hands into the pockets of his blue chinos. "I'm also meeting the suits leasing my oil rich land later so I thought I'd leave the battered boots and old jeans at home."

"And your Stetson?"

Clint's eyes crinkled at the corners. "In my car."

He gestured to a fancy SUV across the road, solidly black and engineered in Germany.

Nice wheels. "Where's the beloved rust bucket?"

"In for repairs."

Fee wrinkled her nose. "Tell me what it costs and I'll pay."

"Don't worry about it."

"Clint, I damaged it, I need to pay for those damages."

Clint surprised her with his quiet okay. "It won't be twenty grand," he added.

"What a shock," Fee replied, her tone dry. She saw his mouth kick up in a half smile and her ovaries quivered.

I want him. Again. Some more. A lot more.

Calm down, Martinez, you fool. That ship has sailed. Wanting to get her mind off the fact that Clint had seen her naked, and that she wanted him to see her naked again, and vice versa, she glanced at the half-constructed building.

"What are you building here?" Fee asked, rubbing her hands on her arms, conscious that the wind had picked up and that it was on the wrong side of chilly.

Clint, being the observant soldier he was, noticed her shivers, pulled off his sweater and placed the opening over her head. Fee didn't argue, she was grateful to be warm, and threaded her arms through the sleeves, rolling back the excess material. "Thank you."

"Pleasure. This wind is picking up," Clint commented, looking at the swaying trees to the side of the building.

"Isn't that what wind does?" Fee asked, confused.

Clint looked down at her. "Farmers don't like wind, especially not when it's dry. It just takes a stray spark and the right wind and we're in trouble, fire wise."

Oh. That made sense. Fee nodded to the building. "So, this?"

Clint placed his hand on her back and Fee forced herself not to react, not to move closer so she could soak up his heat or inhale more of his aftershave.

"It's a new fire station. The old one is too small, too cramped and too outdated."

"And why are you here, having on-site meetings?"

"I spent some time in California, ages ago, doing a smoke jumping and firefighting course. Because nobody in Royal forgets anything, I ended up coordinating Roya's firefighting efforts. It's my contribution to the community," Clint told her. His small, sexy smile flickered. "I do, occasionally, interact with the folks of Royal."

But only on his terms. And he was fudging, she could tell. "I still don't understand why you were having an intense discussion with the architects."

She saw him flush, felt his hand drop away. Rockwell didn't like talking about himself, didn't like anyone seeing below the surface. But he wasn't difficult to figure out.

"Just admit it, Rockwell, you're building this fire

station," Fee stated, her tone brooking no argument. "From your own pockets, I presume?"

"Yep," Clint eventually replied, lifting his shoulders in a casual shrug.

"Those are pretty deep pockets, Clint," Fee murmured, impressed. Knowing there was more to this story, she pushed. "What else are you funding?"

Clint narrowed his eyes at her. "That's none of your business."

"Fire trucks? Water tankers? New equipment?"

Clint rolled his eyes. "If I say yes, will you shut up?"

She grinned, enjoying his discomfort. "What else? New uniforms, a secretary, hmm, maybe some permanent staff since I've heard the town uses volunteers?"

"All of the above and two helicopters outfitted with the latest firefighting and crime-fighting tech—so the police can use them too," Clint admitted, sounding resigned. He stared up at the bright blue sky and shook his head. "It's something I've been working on since I returned home. How the hell do you get me to tell you stuff I don't tell anyone else?"

"It's a skill," Fee said, sounding, and feeling, smug.

"War hero, rich, sexy as hell and generous," Fee added. "You are too much, Rockwell."

"I'm not a hero. I have the money and I'm sure as hell not sexy."

He uttered those words with complete conviction. Fee shook her head in disbelief. She met his eyes and arched her eyebrows. "Did we not have this conversation? Did I not see you naked?"

Clint rubbed the back of his neck. "Holy crap, Martinez, stop."

"Why?" Fee demanded, wanting to see what he'd do, whether he was going to slam his mouth on hers, like they both were desperate for him to do. Dammit, the attraction hadn't faded; they still wanted each other as much as before.

"I want some more naked time, with you," Fee stated, holding his eye.

And her breath.

"Another one-night stand?"

Fee just nodded, unable to talk for once, since her heart sat on her tongue.

Clint looked at his watch and took forever to answer. "I have an appointment now but I can reschedule."

It was tempting—it really was. Fee was considering whether she could duck out of her commitments when Clint's phone jangled. He cursed before pulling it from the back pocket of his pants. Frowning, he quickly answered the call and his terse one-word replies gave her no hint of the subject of the conversation. Clint finished his call, told her he needed a rain check and started to walk toward his SUV across the road.

"What's the matter?" Fee demanded, walking quickly to match his long stride.

"There was a lightning strike yesterday and it set some land alight on the outskirts of town. We thought we had it under control but it sparked up again and if we don't get it under control quickly, it can become a big problem," Clint replied, sounding terse.

"Because of these winds, right?"

Clint nodded and pulled his keys from the pocket of his chinos. "I'm going to head over there, assess the situation, decide whether we need more people to fight it. So, about that rain check?"

It wasn't the right time to discuss this, he was in a hurry, but she didn't want him to think there was a possibility of anything growing between them. This was just about a passionate attraction, she was leaving soon.

She always left…

"We're still ships passing in the night, right?"

Clint cupped her jaw, ran his thumb across her lower lip. "I kind of think we're still in the harbor, on furlough, needing to have some fun before we both move on. Can I call you?"

They exchanged numbers and Fee sighed when Clint's lips met hers in a hard, passion-filled kiss. He pulled back and cursed. "I shouldn't, I don't have time but…hell."

He gathered her close, kissed her thoroughly, his tongue sliding into her mouth as if he owned it. Fee didn't mind, she was happy to stand on any pavement, anywhere being kissed by this man.

The sound of a honking car broke their kiss and Fee heard catcalls and whistles and the rich laughter of four elderly women slowly driving past. Fee, mortified, closed her eyes and wondered how long it would take for this news to hit the gossip airwaves. Ten seconds? Twenty?

"Well, that's going to cause some talk," Clint said.

Fee winced and stepped back. "Sorry."

Clint sent her a rare smile. "Worth it," he said, before climbing into his SUV and driving off.

The fire on the edge of town was under control... not extinguished but under control. Clint stamped on a burning tuft of grass as he retreated toward the road, watching the other firefighters with a critical eye. They had all worked like fiends and he was grateful for their effort since this was a volunteer gig.

As he had back in the unit, Clint felt himself taking command, keeping an eye out, feeling responsible for all the men and women who'd pulled on the safety gear he'd donated and gone out to beat back the fire threatening the houses and land on the west side of town. Somehow, because of his military training, he'd become their temporary Fire Chief. He was proud of Royal, proud of the residents and proud they were prepared to get their hands dirty.

It was nearly over and they could soon go home.

Clint turned at the beep of a horn and sighed when he saw the van pull to a stop behind the cordon. The exhale turned into a muttered curse when he saw those spectacular legs, those black curls. Fee was now dressed in black designer jeans and knee-high heeled boots and wore a thigh-length leather jacket over a white silk top. He'd give her ten minutes, tops, before the flying soot stained it beyond repair.

Clint narrowed his eyes as two men also jumped out of the van, cameras on their shoulders. Fee spoke to one cameraman, her eyes moving from the camera to the swathe of burned land beyond the cordon. She pointed to where the fire stopped on the edge of Mrs. McPherson's garden and her hands moved as fast as her mouth. He wondered what she was saying.

They started to move in his direction and Clint swallowed a curse. He glanced back at his crew, then turned to face Fee and the dreaded cameras.

"Don't have time for this, Martinez."

"Two minutes, Rockwell," Fee said, holding up her finger. "Is everything okay?"

Clint nodded "Yeah, mostly."

"Mostly?"

"There are still a couple of spots burning. We're working on them," Clint said, his tone terse. He felt a fresh gust on his cheek and frowned. The wind had died down ten minutes ago but it was picking up again. He looked around, saw wind whipping the trees and released a series of violent, army-based curses.

Fee reached across the cordon to lay her hand on the yellow sleeve of his fire jacket. "Clint? What is it?"

"The wind has changed direction and is strengthening. If we don't kill the fire now, we're going to have a helluva problem on our hands. We need more hands, and we need them quickly."

Fee handed her microphone to the cameraman— Jimmy?—and spread her hands. "Let me help."

Clint frowned at her. "What?"

Fee pointed to a firefighter who was smacking the grass with the back of a shovel. "I can do that. I want to help. And you just said you need hands."

He did. Not to mention, Fee was wearing her stubborn face and he didn't have time to argue. He wasn't about to put her to work fighting flames—hell to the no!—but there were other ways she could help. He thought for a moment. If the fire turned and started heading back in the direction of the houses, they could find themselves in a world of trouble.

"I need you to go down this street, go house to house and ask the residents to prepare to vacate their houses. I don't want to create a panic—it's a precautionary measure. Make a list of who will go, who won't and get it back to me as soon as possible. Note down any injuries, any sick people, anyone who needs special care. Basically, anybody who can't move fast."

Fee nodded. "Sure, I can do that for you. Where will you be?"

Clint gestured to a strip of flames to the east of the original fire and sighed. "There. Hang around once you've gotten your list. If I need your information, I'll find you."

"Okay." Fee grabbed his hand and squeezed. "Be safe."

Another hard kiss and she didn't seem to mind that his face was covered in grime, that he smelled of fire and smoke and burned grass. "You too. And thanks. I appreciate you pitching in."

Fee smiled. "Hey, the sooner we get this done, the sooner we can play our ships game again. Hurry the hell up."

Clint smiled and then laughed.

Fee was, at the very least, entertaining.

The small fire turned into something bigger than he'd expected, but six hours later they'd managed to contain the blaze. While it wasn't the hardest challenge he'd ever faced, it had been a long day. He was desperate to get home, take off his prosthetic, slide into his tub and stay there until his muscles were lax and his washing-machine brain stopped churning.

Clint walked toward his vehicle and pulled off his jacket. He ran his forearm over his filthy face, grimacing at the streaks of dirt covering his arm. He'd have to take a shower before he sank into his tub. Man, he couldn't wait to get home. Clint looked around, saw many of his crew were also stripping down, guzzling water, all looking tired and played out. The *Secret Lives* van was gone and Clint sighed at his surge of disappointment.

Fee had, obviously, left as well.

Good thing he hadn't needed the list of evacuees from her. *Dammit, Fee, I trusted you with a task and when you got bored, you bailed. What if I had needed that information, what then?*

Annoyed with her, and with himself for believing in her, he flipped open the back door of his SUV and pulled out a cooler. Slamming the lid up, he yanked out a bottle of cold water and furiously cracked the top. This was why he shouldn't trust people, why he should keep to himself, be alone. Because people always, always let you down.

"Can I have one of those?"

Clint lowered the bottle from his mouth and turned around slowly, his eyes widening at the sight of the tiny figure in the fire suit. Her hair hung in strings down her face and her face was as dirty as his, possibly dirtier. The blue rings under her eyes told him she was beyond exhausted.

It looked like she'd been fighting the fire but that was impossible because he was in charge and he hadn't authorized her to fight the goddamn fire! He was going to find the person who put her out there and string him up by his balls! How dare he put her in danger?

"What the hell, Fee?" he roared, causing heads to turn and eyebrows to raise.

"You needed help, I helped," Fee said, placing her hands on her lower back and stretching. Her fire jacket hung past her knees and her boots were at least two sizes too big for her. "And, before you erupt like a volcano, I wasn't in any danger. I just went over ground the guys had already cleared, making doubly sure there were no sparks."

Okay, relief. Maybe he wouldn't have to kill any of his volunteers today.

"Still not happy," he told her, rubbing her cheekbone with his thumb. But he was relieved to know she hadn't bailed and that she'd taken his request to stick around seriously.

"I appreciate your willingness to help, Seraphina,

I do. But I didn't know you were in the field and that's a problem. Firstly, because I need to know exactly who I'm responsible for so I can ensure that the head count I had at the beginning is accurate, that the people who walked into the path of the fire are the people who walked out. If you got into trouble, I wouldn't have known to even look for you."

"Dav—" Fee winced as she let slip the name of the volunteer who'd allowed her to work. Clint would deal with him later. "He knew I was there."

"And if he got into trouble and couldn't tell me?" Clint asked, trying to keep his tone conversational. He was trying to be reasonable, reminding himself she was a civilian and he couldn't rip her a new one like he would one of his unit.

She'd also, he admitted, had the best intentions at heart and didn't know any better. Still, she'd never learn if no one told her, so he continued his lecture.

"I have to take every variable into account, think ten steps ahead. And I needed to know where you were in case the fire got out of control and headed for the houses. You had information I might've needed."

"I knew where you were every minute," Fee said, lifting her chin. "I watched you, and I would've known if you were looking for me."

Well, that was something. And, really, they were arguing—discussing—a possibility that hadn't, thankfully, materialized. And she had pitched in, gotten dirty, shed her socialite skin to help when help was needed. He admired and respected her for it.

Clint handed her his all but full bottle of water. "Drink. And when you're done, drink some more."

"Aye, aye, Lieutenant."

"Smart-ass," Clint muttered as he reached for another bottle.

Fee's eyes twinkled at him. "I thought you rather liked my ass."

He did. And every other inch of her body. Fee chugged back her water, wiping her mouth when she was done and creating a new streak of dirt across her chin.

He grinned and shook his head. "You are something else, Seraphina Martinez."

"I know," Fee replied, her tone jaunty. She arched a thin, dirty eyebrow. "Think you can handle me, Rockwell?"

"I never start something I can't finish, Martinez," Clint said, not caring the local media were milling about. He'd spotted a cameraman from a nearby TV station hovering around earlier but that didn't stop him from reaching for the zipper on her fire suit and pulling it down.

Fee just laughed. "I wouldn't do that, cowboy."

"And why not?"

Fee laughed at him. "Look down."

Clint looked at her chest and saw she was only wearing another sexy bra. This one was lacy and transparent and the color of a tangerine. His mouth, dry from the fire, felt like it hadn't tasted water in years. He looked again, he couldn't not, and zipped her up.

"Why aren't you wearing anything under your jacket?" he asked, sounding like someone had a very strong pair of hands around his throat.

Fee looked at him as if he'd lost his mind. "Because I was a wearing a very expensive designer silk shirt and it would not survive the soot and dirt." She grinned at him. "You see, I was taking all the variables into account, thinking ten steps ahead."

"As I said, smart-ass."

"Yeah, but you like it."

God help him, he did. And, this time, he wasn't only talking about her very fine butt.

Six

They stripped off in the mudroom off Clint's kitchen and walked through his lovely house in their underwear. Fee was quite glad Clint held her hand and led the way; she wasn't sure whether she'd be able to find his bedroom again in the ridiculously large-for-one-person house.

Fee glanced through open doors as he tugged her along past a library, a study, a sunroom, a kick-ass media-slash-theater room. Another sitting room.

They all but sprinted past the gym containing the massage table where he'd made love to her. At the end of one wing, separate from the rest of the house, Clint pulled her into his bedroom and, once again, she looked around, enjoying the masculine space. The walls and floors were finished to look like con-

crete and two massive frames, splitting the canvas
with a view of a snow-covered mountain, formed the
headboard. The room itself was a study in gray and
neutral colors but the focal point was the floor-to-
ceiling views out over the paddocks to where Clint's
award-winning Appaloosas grazed.

It suddenly occurred to Fee that they'd made love
in this bed where anyone approaching the paddock
could see them.

"While I'm not a prude, I don't feel comfortable
standing in front of the window, dressed like this.
Or naked."

Clint's teeth flashed white in his soot-covered
face. "We can see out, they can't see in."

Thank God. There was reality TV and then there
was providing sex shows to Clint's ranch hands. In
her book, that was a step, or five hundred, too far.

"Let's get you cleaned up, Seraphina," Clint said,
leading her into his gray-and-black bathroom. Stepping into the massive shower cubicle, he flipped the
taps to one of the two shower heads and gestured
her inside. "Take your time, there's plenty of water."

Fee immediately sensed he was uncomfortable. She
saw a pair of crutches within easy reach of the shower
stall and noticed the wooden bench running the length
of the massive shower. She glanced at his prosthetic
and realized Clint would have to remove it to shower.
With all its electronics, it couldn't be waterproof.

She'd finally see him without his bionic leg. The
last time they made love, he hadn't removed it but
it was time. Fee tipped her head to one side and

handed him a gentle smile. "Come and shower with me, Rockwell."

Clint looked indecisive and she could see the excuse on his lips. "Clint, c'mon. I'm dead on my feet and we can kill two birds with one stone. We can get clean together and have some fun."

"I—"

Fee placed her hand on his bare chest and sighed. "We've been over this, Rockwell. I'm not going to faint and run screaming into the night. Trust me, just a little."

Clint scowled and stared at the stream of water falling inside the cubicle. When he cursed and sat down on the bench outside the shower, she knew she had won. The trick was, Fee decided, not to let him see a hint of surprise, a smidgen of doubt. If he did, he'd rabbit and they'd be back to square one.

She needed to distract him so she bent her head for a kiss. Clint pulled back from her and grimaced. "I'm filthy, Fee."

"So am I." She smiled against his lips. "I don't think I've ever been this dirty in my life but it's good dirt, you know? Dirt gathered while I did something important…or am I being silly?"

"I understand exactly what you mean," Clint replied, his eyes serious. "Good dirt is the sweat and dust after rounding up cattle, after spending the day checking fences, training horses."

"It's strange but nice," Fee said. Hearing the release of air, she looked down. Clint's bionic leg was in his hand and she could finally see what was left of his leg. Dropping to her haunches, she examined his injury. The top of his thigh was pure muscle, right down to where his leg ended, an inch or two above his knee. There were scars, sure, lots of them but…

It wasn't a big deal. It wasn't ugly or pretty or strange or unusual, it was…it just was. It was Clint. Fee risked placing her hand over the end of his leg, gently squeezed it and stood up. Handing him a crutch, she quickly stripped out of her underwear and ducked under the spray, groaning as she tipped her face up to receive the hot water.

Bliss.

After a minute, she opened her eyes and looked at Clint, who looked shocked. She was not going to make this a big deal, because it wasn't. "Are you coming in? Because, you know, over here, I've got soap and skin and shower sex just waiting for you."

Clint gestured to the crutch tucked under his arm. "That's going to have to wait until I get you in my bed."

Fee ignored the tremble in his voice. God, some-one had really done a number on his head. "Oh, we'll get to the bed but there's a bench in here. I rather fancy sitting on your lap…"

Clint groaned and pushed his boxer briefs down with one hand. "At the risk of repeating myself, you are something else, Seraphina Martinez."

Fee shot him a naughty grin. "So I've been told."

Turning as he stepped into the cubicle, she flipped on the other shower head and water pounded them from every direction. Fee felt like a dozen hands were massaging her muscles. "Oh, this is fabulous. I want a shower like this."

Clint pulled her to him, aligning their bodies so she was plastered against him, skin to skin. Fee ignored his crutch and lifted her hands to cup his face.

"You did good work today, Rockwell," she said, loving the gold in his hazel eyes. Gold meant he was turned on, feeling relaxed. Green was his hiding-from-the-world color. When his eyes turned gray, as they did earlier when he heard she'd been fighting the fire, she knew he was angry.

He was such a protector, such an alpha male. God, she adored him.

Shaking off the unsettling thought that she was allowing Clint to sneak too far under her skin, Fee lifted her mouth for a kiss and sighed when he covered her lips with his. Passion sparked, flared and exploded. His tongue wound around hers, demanding that she keep up as he feasted on her mouth. Fee fell, whirling and swirling, into this magical world he created, allowing their mutual fascination to take her on a magic carpet ride.

This was as close to love as she'd ever felt since those first heady days with her ex. A little scared but a lot turned on, Fee ran her hands down his sides, across his hard stomach and down to capture his hard cock between her hands. He used his free hand to hold one breast, his thumb swiping her nipple before running the backs of his fingers down her ribcage, and down her hip to a small patch of hair at the top of her sex. Then his long fingers parted her, tested her, and she whimpered as her magic carpet lifted her higher. Clint found her bundle of nerves and gently, so gently, stroked her. Fee dropped her forehead onto his sternum, panting softly. There were so many sensations hitting her—the hot, hard streams of water, the sooty scent of his fabulous skin, the harshness of his ragged breath as she stroked him from base to tip, his warm mouth on the ball of her shoulder.

It was all too much, too intense. She was so close and, judging by his soft curses and the urgency with which he thrust into her fist, so was he.

Fee let out a whimper as he slid a finger into her, then another and she released a low scream when he curled his fingers to hit a spot deep inside her. His thumb brushed her clit and she moaned against his chest, instinctively increasing the pressure on his cock, rubbing her thumb across the head every time he thrust his hips into her hard grip.

"So close, Fee," Clint muttered.

"Me too."

"Fly, sweetheart." Clint tapped her inner walls and Fee, flying on her magic carpet, hit the sun and shattered into a million sunbeams. From somewhere far away she realized Clint had also found his release and it felt like they were dancing on the rainbow, riding streams of sunlight.

The rainbow slowly disappeared and gray tiles and black walls replaced the shimmery sunbeams. Eventually, Fee blinked, realizing she had collapsed against Clint who, in turn, was using the wall to hold up their combined weight. He still held his crutch under one arm but the other was wrapped around her back, holding her tight. The side of his face rested on the top of her head.

"What the hell was that?" Clint muttered.

"Mutual madness," Fee sleepily replied. Now, if he could wash her, dress her and let her sleep, that would be great.

"Well said." Clint lifted his head up. Fee managed to raise her own head to smile at him.

"Was that amazingly good or was that just me?"

"It was good," Clint responded, dropping a quick kiss on her lips. He touched her lips with his fingers before pushing some wet curls off her forehead. "Let's get you clean and dressed, Martinez, and I'll see what I can heat up for supper."

Fee yawned and reached for the loofah and soap. "Don't worry about food. I'm too exhausted to eat."

"Food, then sleep."

"Sleep, then more sex—we can skip the food."

Clint smiled at her and her stomach rolled over. Really, the man should smile more since his smiles had the power to light up the sun. "I know my housekeeper cooked up some mole poblano earlier today."

Fee narrowed her eyes at him in mock outrage. "You're trying to tempt me to eat using Mexican food?"

"Well…yeah."

Fee was suddenly ravenous. "Well, it worked. I adore mole. Let's get clean and eat. Okay, new plan, food, sex and sleep."

Clint sent her a look of mock horror. "Woman, you're insatiable."

She needed to remind them why they were here, what they were doing. "Well, if this is just our furlough together then I've got to get in as much as I can before I leave. Don't you agree?"

Clint's eyes took on a hint of green. "Absolutely." He reached for the shampoo and, using the wall for balance, dolloped some into his hand. "Because we're both not looking for a relationship."

Fee stared down at her pink toes. Exactly.

Because she wasn't...

Was she?

It was past midnight and Fee had yet to fall asleep. The moon was high in the sky and provided them with enough light to pick up the movement of the wind blowing in the trees, the individual slats of the white paddock fences.

It was a stunning night and if she only had a little time with Clint, she didn't want to waste it sleeping.

"Are you asleep?" Fee whispered, her words bouncing off Clint's chest. Her head was on his shoulder, her thigh rested across his leg, her knee tucked into it. She'd never felt so comfortable, so at peace, in her life.

"Nah. But if you want more sex, I doubt I can oblige. I'm done."

Fee doubted that. She was sure she could persuade him but she was too relaxed to make the effort. She just wanted to lie here, in his big arms, feeling happy and relaxed and, yes, protected.

Despite having parents, she'd been—mentally and

emotionally—on her own for most of her life and she could count, on one hand, the number of people with whom she could fully relax. But Clint made her feel more than relaxed; he made her feel safe, like trouble would have to go through him before reaching her.

It was both a heady and a dangerous feeling. She couldn't allow herself to get used to it. She was leaving, sometime soon after the New Year's Eve bash at the famous, original TCC clubhouse. Within days she'd be gone and Clint would be nothing more than a delicious memory.

"I can hear you thinking," Clint said, his fingers running up and down her spine.

She couldn't tell him the truth so she hunted for another subject. "Did you ever think about following your mom into journalism?"

Clint tensed. "Hell, no."

Fee frowned, remembering she'd seen footage of him on one of his mom's shows. The research she'd done on him since their first time together had been extensive. And, no, she wasn't creepy. Or weird.

Just curious.

She might as well be upfront about it. "I like to know with whom I'm sleeping so I did a little research on you. For someone with no social media presence, there's a lot about you on the 'net."

Clint answered with a sleepy "yeah" but didn't sound like he cared much.

"I watched some old reruns of your mom's show. She often talks about you. She's even shown videos of your graduation ceremony and some from your

Dear Reader,

Since you are a lover of our books, your opinions are important to us... and so is your time.

That's why we made sure your **"FAST FIVE" READER SURVEY** can be completed in just a few minutes. Your answers to the five questions will help us remain at the forefront of women's fiction.

And, as a thank-you for participating, we'd like to send you **4 FREE THANK-YOU GIFTS!**

Enjoy your gifts with our appreciation,

Pam Powers

To get your
4 FREE THANK-YOU GIFTS:

✳ Quickly complete the "Fast Five" Reader Survey
and return the insert.

▲ DETACH AND MAIL CARD TODAY! ▼

"FAST FIVE" READER SURVEY

1 Do you sometimes read a book a second or third time? ○ Yes ○ No

2 Do you often choose reading over other forms of entertainment such as television? ○ Yes ○ No

3 When you were a child, did someone regularly read aloud to you? ○ Yes ○ No

4 Do you sometimes take a book with you when you travel outside the home? ○ Yes ○ No

5 In addition to books, do you regularly read newspapers and magazines? ○ Yes ○ No

YES! I have completed the above Reader Survey. Please send me my 4 FREE GIFTS (gifts worth over $20 retail). I understand that I am under no obligation to buy anything, as explained on the back of this card.

225/326 HDL GNQC

FIRST NAME	LAST NAME

ADDRESS

APT.#	CITY

STATE/PROV.	ZIP/POSTAL CODE

© 2019 HARLEQUIN ENTERPRISES LIMITED
® and ™ are trademarks owned and used by the trademark owner and/or its licensee. Printed in the U.S.A.

READER SERVICE—here's how it works:

Accepting your 2 free Harlequin Desire® books and 2 free gifts (gifts valued at approximately $10.00 retail) places you under no obligation to buy anything. You may keep the books and gifts and return the shipping statement marked "cancel." If you do not cancel, about a month later we'll send you 6 additional books and bill you just $4.55 each in the U.S. or $5.24 each in Canada. That is a savings of at least 13% off the cover price. It's quite a bargain! Shipping and handling is just 50¢ per book in the U.S. and $1.25 per book in Canada*. You may cancel at any time, but if you choose to continue, every month we'll send you 6 more books, which you may either purchase at the discount price plus shipping and handling or return to us and cancel your subscription.
*Terms and prices subject to change without notice. Prices do not include sales taxes which will be charged (if applicable) based on your state or country of residence. Canadian residents will be charged applicable taxes. Offer not valid in Quebec. Books received may not be as shown. All orders subject to approval. Credit or debit balances in a customer's account(s) may be offset by any other outstanding balance owed by or to the customer. Please allow 3 to 4 weeks for delivery. Offer available while quantities last.

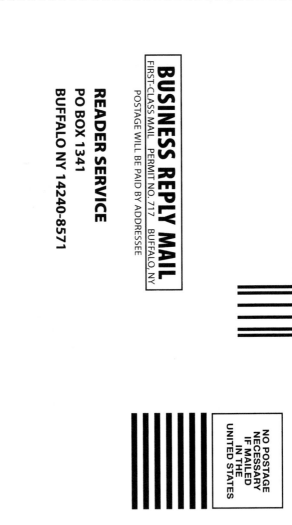

◄ If offer card is missing write to: Reader Service, P.O. Box 1341, Buffalo, NY 14240-8531 or visit www.ReaderService.com ◄

BUSINESS REPLY MAIL
FIRST-CLASS MAIL   PERMIT NO. 717   BUFFALO, NY

POSTAGE WILL BE PAID BY ADDRESSEE

READER SERVICE
PO BOX 1341
BUFFALO NY 14240-8571

NO POSTAGE
NECESSARY
IF MAILED
IN THE
UNITED STATES

childhood. She spoke about you often during her series about wounded soldiers and their heroism. They
were heart-wrenching and rather wonderful."

"Yeah, my mom is a great BS artist."

Fee pulled her head off his chest to look up into
his hard eyes. "What do you mean by *that*?"

Clint's sigh whispered over her hair. "My mom
talks a good line but she doesn't like getting her
hands dirty. Her sympathy and her patriotic spirit
are all BS. She doesn't care about me, or about any
of the veterans she interviewed for that series. She's
all about her ratings and understands that wounded
soldiers are a great way to get viewers."

He made the harsh statement in an ordering-coffee
voice and Fee knew that she had to choose her next
words carefully. "How do you know that, Clint?"

"Because she was in my room after I had my leg
amputated and I overheard her telling her manager
that I repulsed her. That she liked pretty and she
liked perfect and I didn't hit either mark anymore.
And she was happy I had a massive trust fund to
fund me and a girlfriend to nurse me because she
had no intention of helping my suddenly incapable
ass." His voice was rough with disappointment and
anger. "And I realized that if she couldn't care about
me, how much can she care about the other vets?"

God, that explained so much. Fee suddenly understood why he was so independent, why he pushed
himself so hard. It made her heart ache for him even
as she reeled at his mother's callous attitude. While

her parents had been a tad neglectful and a lot self-absorbed, they were never cruel.

His mother was a witch of epic proportions. "Man, that's cold."

Clint's fingers dug into her spine. "She really is. She's all about the packaging, not the gift."

"Is she the reason you keep to yourself, why you don't interact much with people? Why you don't... date?"

Fee knew there was more to his story, a lot more, and she wanted to know every detail.

"As I said, I had a girlfriend when I returned home," he admitted. "We'd been together for a while, but after the surgery, she moved in. She really looked after me. Saw to my every need...except one."

Fee winced. "Sex?"

"Yep."

Ah, no.

"She couldn't, with me, and after she left, I tried to date but that didn't turn out so well. So, I figured it was easier not to."

No wonder he'd had doubts about her reaction to seeing him naked. Who wouldn't?

"Between my mother and my ex and my inability to get lucky, I kind of lost my faith in people after that. I suppose that's also why I avoided Royal and people in general. I hate feeling less than, weak, incapable, disabled."

Fee tightened her arm across his chest and kissed his shoulder.

"I vowed I would do everything and anything I

was able to do before. And I vowed I would never let anyone see me as anything other than fully capable."

And that was why he never allowed anyone to see his fake leg, to see him using crutches, to view him as being disabled. Because he wasn't disabled. He was one of the most able people she knew. "You've just lost half of your leg, that's all. To me it's no more important than a scar or a birthmark. It's a part of you but it doesn't define you."

Clint didn't reply—she hadn't expected him to— but she felt his appreciation in the way he tightened his grip on her, in the way he rested his lips in her hair. It was all she needed.

Clint's voice, when he spoke again minutes later, was rough with emotion. "How was your Christmas, by the way? Where did you go?"

Back on stable conversational ground. "I went to see my folks, in Florida. I gave them a cruise for Christmas, they gave me a voucher from Target. My mom bitched about my antics on *Secret Lives*, I tried to explain, again, that the show is scripted, that I'm playing a part. She doesn't get it."

"Not much reality in reality TV, huh?"

"Not so much, no," Fee replied. "But it's provided me with a healthy nest egg and a platform. I'm thinking about writing another cookbook, maybe trying to get a gig as a celebrity chef when the show ends."

"You cook?"

"I cook damn well," Fee told him. "I spent a lot of my childhood comfort eating and I wanted to learn how to make the foods I loved. We moved around too much for me to be able to revisit favorite restaurants or bakeries so I had to figure out how to cook everything myself. I make a mean red velvet cupcake and my fish tacos are to die for."

Clint moaned. "I love fish tacos." He pulled away from her to lie on his side, his head resting in his hand, facing her. "Why did you comfort eat?"

Time for her to get personal. Fee thought it wasn't clever to be exchanging confidences when she was leaving—but then, maybe that was what made it okay. In a few weeks, he'd just be a lovely memory, so what was the harm in telling him things she'd never told anyone before?

"We moved a lot and there was a new school— sometimes more than one—every year. Coming into a new school as a fat Latina was like putting a bull's-eye on your head and handing the kids a bow and arrow. I learned to fade into the walls, to make myself as invisible as possible. Even if I'd wanted to make friends, it wouldn't have been easy. And I didn't want to. Getting attached meant getting hurt… I don't allow myself to become attached, Clint."

"Because it hurts too much when you leave. And you always leave."

She nodded. "I tried to tell my parents I was unhappy, but they brushed me off. I told school counselors, and they did the bare minimum, which basically amounted to nothing."

Fee rested her head on the pillow, her hand on his chest. "I desperately wanted a stable base as a child but thanks to the way I grew up, I was equally terrified of being trapped. While I was going through hell at one school or another, the only way to survive was to believe I was only there for a set time, that the next school, town, situation would be better. I built up this idea that the grass is always greener just around the corner."

Clint stroked her from shoulder to hand and back up again. "Parents and the many ways they manage to mess with their kids' heads."

"Do you want kids, Clint?" Fee sleepily asked.

"Yeah, sort of. Bit difficult to do when I'm not so keen on the wife and the relationship that goes along with them. You?"

Fee yawned. "Sort of, for the same reasons." Her eyes drifted close. "I'm so tired, Clint."

Clint's fingers drifted across her jaw. "Then sleep, sweetheart. I've got you."

He did, but just for tonight. Because that was all she had, all she was allowed.

Situated in Royal, The Bellamy was the establishment all Fee's future visits to hotels would be measured against. Sitting on fifty or more acres of ruthless landscaping and lavish gardens, it had more than two hundred lusciously appointed suites, containing every gadget known to man. As well as staying at the resort while in Royal, she and her friends had been filmed dancing, and drinking, in The Silver Saddle bar and eating tapas from their award-winning menu. They'd eaten at the hotel's amazing farm-to-table restaurant The Glass House and today they were going to be filmed enjoying a spa day at Pure.

The Bellamy had it all.

After a night long on sex and short on sleep, Fee hoped she wouldn't snooze her way through the filming.

Deciding she needed coffee—preferably intravenously injected—she popped into the small, intimate coffee shop to the left of the dining room and smiled when she saw Lulu sitting at a small table by the French doors, scrolling through her phone. Kace LeBlanc sat at the table next to hers, reading a newspaper, and they were both studiously, deliberately ignoring each other.

What was their problem?

Pulling out a chair opposite Lu, Fee sat down, reached for Lu's coffee mug and took a large sip. Black and sweet, just the way she liked it.

"Hey!" Lu complained, her head jerking up.

"I need it," Fee told her, taking another drink. When the waitress approached them, she quickly ordered a stack of pancakes and a cup of coffee of her own.

"Nigel will freak if you put on weight," Lulu pointed out.

Fee smirked. "I worked it off last night and I'll go for a run later."

"God, I hate you," Lulu told her, raising her voice so the next part could be heard clear across the room. "I think I'm a born-again virgin, it's been so long."

Because Lulu was rarely so brash, and never at that volume, Fee quickly realized she was trying to make Kace feel uncomfortable. Fee darted a look at him but the man gave no indication he was listening to their conversation.

"I'm so jealous," Lulu told her. "I still haven't bagged a cowboy of my own."

Kace abruptly stood up and threw his linen napkin onto the table. They both watched as he quietly and deliberately folded his newspaper before finally tucking it under his arm. When he lifted his head, he only had eyes for Lulu.

"Can you, possibly, drop the reality star persona for five seconds?"

Lulu draped an elegant arm over the back of her chair. It was no accident that the movement made her chest lift. Kace's eyes dropped and he looked his fill. He shook his head when their gazes clashed again. "Like what you see, LeBlanc?"

"Any man with a pulse would," Kace replied. "But that's all surface, Ms. Sheppard. Is there anything beneath your pretty exterior? Like a brain? Or a heart?"

Lulu's eyes narrowed and Fee leaned back. She'd experienced Lulu's temper before and Kace was in her firing line. But instead of unloading, Lulu just stared at him with wide, round, hurt, eyes.

Worried that Lulu was genuinely upset, Fee opened her mouth to defend her friend against the stuffy lawyer, prepared to rip his heart out. But Lu shook her head and Fee shut her mouth.

Lulu had this.

One tear, perfect and devastating, rolled down Lulu's cheek. Fee hid her smile knowing Lulu could cry on demand and did it oh, so well. Lulu blinked, allowing another two tears to roll down her face.

"That's such a hurtful thing to say," Lulu whispered, her hand on her heart.

Instead of falling to his knees and begging her forgiveness, LeBlanc just arched one eyebrow, his brown eyes cool. "Cut the crap, Ms. Sheppard, your tears don't fool me."

Fee gasped, then winced. Nobody, and especially no man, had ever looked past Lu's tears. When she turned on the waterworks, every single one of them had begged for her forgiveness.

Huh.

So maybe the stuffy lawyer could see past Lu's particular brand of BS.

Lu's tears instantly cleared. "Well, well, well… you aren't just a pretty face."

Lulu resumed her languid, arm-over-the-back-of-her-chair pose. She crossed one long, gorgeous leg over the other and tipped her head to one side. "What is your problem, LeBlanc? With me, specifically?"

Kace shook his head. "Dammit, you're gorgeous. But you're also vain and superficial and shallow."

"So decisive in your opinions and we haven't even had a proper conversation," Lulu drawled. "Well, if we're making snap judgments, you're buttoned up, stuffy and have a stick up your ass."

Kace sent her a tight smile. "Glad to have that cleared up." Picking up his briefcase, he abruptly turned and marched out of the coffee shop.

Because she admired the back view of a built guy as much as the next girl, Fee sighed. "He's seriously hot."

Lulu reached across the table and pinched the skin on the back of her hand. Fee yelped and jerked her hand away. "What is wrong with you?"

"He's annoying, and stuffy, and condescending and annoying—"

"You said that."

"—and patronizing and buttoned up and very, very annoying."

"You're repeating yourself," Fee said, enjoying herself hugely. Lulu usually had men eating out of her hand and it was fun watching her deal with the one man who refused to grovel at her admittedly beautiful feet.

"You're attracted to him," she added.

"I. Am. Not," Lulu told her through gritted teeth.

"And you both love and hate the fact he's not super impressed by you."

Lulu glared at her. "Stop. Talking."

"You want what you can't have," Fee said, risking her friend's legendary temper.

"I hate you so much right now."

Fee leaned back as the waitress placed her plate in front of her. When the girl was gone, she dug into her pancakes.

"And you're jealous I spent the night having spectacular sex and you…didn't." Come to think of it, that really was strange. Even if she was trading barbs with the stuck-up lawyer, Lulu normally, at the very least, had a handful of men wrapped around her baby finger.

Fee chewed, swallowed and waved her fork around. "This town is full of sexy men and you're telling me you haven't managed to date one of them? Why is that, Miss Lulu?"

Lulu picked up a fork and Fee hoped she wouldn't use it as a weapon. "Nobody has caught my eye."

"Oh, someone has caught your eye and you're just pissed you can't bring him to heel, and worse, can't BS him," Fee told her, leaning back as Lu raised her fork. "Don't stab me."

"It's tempting but not today," Lulu retorted. "I am not attracted to LeBlanc. He's so not my type."

Fee hooted, amused. "He's smart, rich and stunningly good-looking. He's *so* your type."

Lulu's fork missed Fee's hand by half an inch and landed in her stack of pancakes. She cut through the fluffy stack with the back of her fork then lifted a huge mouthful and shoved it into her mouth.

Lulu glared at her as she chewed. When she was done, she narrowed her eyes at Fee. "You have me eating pancakes."

"Not me. You always comfort eat when you're upset."

Lulu went back for another bite and Fee whipped her plate away. "Prove LeBlanc didn't upset you by not having another bite."

Lulu held her stare but, after ten seconds, dropped her eyes and waved the waitress over. "Bring me my own pancakes please, heavy on the bacon and the syrup."

"Thought so," Fee said, smirking.

"Fee?" Lulu asked, super sweetly.

"Mmm?"

"Shut. The. Hell. Up."

Seven

What in the name of all things holy was he doing?

Clint stood in front of the door to Fee's home away from home, her suite at The Bellamy, and glared at his highly polished wingtips. He was dressed in a tuxedo, bow tie perfectly knotted, hair brushed and his face clean of its habitual scruff. He'd spent more time dressing for this one night than he had the entire week.

All because Fee had asked him to accompany her to the New Year's Eve ball at the Texas Cattleman's Club. He didn't do balls, the TCC or people, so why on God's great green wonderful earth was he standing outside her hotel door prepared to do all three?

All because a gorgeous brunette with a huge heart and wild curls asked him. And he couldn't blame a post-sex haze for his saying yes. They hadn't even been in the same room. She'd called him up, issued the invitation and he hadn't hesitated.

He was definitely losing his mind.

Clint jammed his hands into the pockets of his tuxedo pants and rocked on his heels. He and Fee had spent all their free time together lately—including very slow horse rides (Fee had never ridden before and was taking forever to learn), quiet dinners and sitting on the porch, drinking wine and talking—and it had been the best time of his life.

The Fee he was coming to know was nothing like the fast-talking, over-the-top character she played on the two episodes of *Secret Lives* he'd managed to watch. Oh, she was a firecracker in either incarnation, and wasn't scared to share her opinions, but one-on-one she was softer and gentler than her on-screen persona.

Clint raked his hand through his hair. She was... amazing.

Uncomfortable with that thought, Clint tried to distract himself by thinking how much had changed, in Royal and in himself.

The Blackwood siblings versus Miranda war was still raging, Kace LeBlanc was still, he presumed, doing what lawyers did to resolve the situation. The *Secret Lives* crew was still milking the drama for reality gold.

All the players in that saga would be present tonight and arguments and snide comments were, as he'd heard from Fee, expected. The situation was tense and everyone was on edge.

Not his problem.

But, at some point the buzz would die down—probably sooner rather than later—and Fee would return to Manhattan. That was a given.

He'd miss her, that much he knew. He also accepted they couldn't have a long-distance relationship. What they had wouldn't survive her leaving Royal. It was a long way from Manhattan to Texas, and if he could barely cope with the small town of Royal, he'd go mad visiting New York.

And, for Fee, Royal was a quirky place to visit but she was too much of a city girl to settle down in a smallish agricultural town.

Not that she had any plans to settle down anywhere. Fee, as she'd told him, liked having options, being able to move on when she needed to. Despite his career in the military, he'd always know he'd return to Royal and his land. He was emotionally tied to his ranch, to his grandfather's and great-grandfather's legacy. He belonged in Texas, on his ranch, raising cattle and horses and avoiding people as much as possible.

They were all the opposites—sun and moon, light and dark, city and country. They didn't have a hailstone's chance in hell of making a relationship work. He didn't want a relationship...

People, he reminded himself, hurt people.

So why was he standing here? Why wasn't he back on the ranch, listening to the wind whistling through the trees, sitting on his porch as one year rolled into another?

Because she'd asked him…

It was a short-term fling, a flash in the pan, a brief, fun affair. There was no need for self-analysis or deep introspection. He wasn't expecting more, neither was she. He was overthinking this…

Just stop, Rockwell. Right damn now.

Annoyed with himself, Clint rapped on the door and heard the click of heels on the tiled floor on the other side of the door. He heard the snick of a lock opening and, when he saw what she was wearing, reached for the doorframe to steady himself.

It was a dress, floor-length, embroidered, with long sleeves, the color of a fiery Rockwell ranch sunset.

The dress plunged to her navel in an enormous V, showing a considerable amount of her fantastic breasts. Clint couldn't decide whether he should rush her downstairs to show her off or take her back inside to see what that dress looked like on the floor. Instead, he just stared at her and reminded himself to breathe. *Holy crap.*

"Hi," Fee said, sounding a little shy. Clint pulled himself together and noticed the hesitancy in her eyes, her need for reassurance. Strange, because he'd never seen her question herself. She'd always seemed to be thoroughly confident in her body.

Could she, possibly, be waiting for his approval, wanting to hear whether he thought she looked good?

She didn't look good—she looked magnificent.

"Uh…um." He could think the words, apparently, but verbalizing them was giving him difficulty.

Fee stroked the lapel of his tuxedo. "You look wonderful, Rockwell. Very debonair."

Say something, dammit. "Thanks. You… Jesus, Fee, that's a helluva dress."

Fee held the edges of the skirt and winced. "Too much?"

He shook his head and ran his finger down the curve of one breast. "Yes, no… My head is spinning."

"In a good or bad way?" Fee asked and he caught her hesitancy again. *Get over yourself, Rockwell.*

Clint held her face in his hands and looked her in the eye. "You look amazing, perfect, gorgeous… too sexy for words. As you might have gathered."

Delight jumped into her brilliant eyes. "Really?"

"Oh, yeah," Clint answered her, looking at her mouth. "Can I kiss you or am I going to find myself wearing your particular shade of lipstick?"

Those plump lips curved up. "It's stay-fast so you should be good."

Clint touched his lips to hers, sighing when she grabbed the lapels of his jacket, holding on while he ravaged her mouth. Yeah, skipping the ball sounded like a fine idea. He'd take his time removing her dress. He'd leave her heels and her dangly earrings on while he kissed her from top to toe…

"Ah, get a room. But later, because we're going to be late."

Clint reluctantly pulled his mouth off Fee's to look over his shoulder at Lulu, who was closing the door to her own suite. She wore an aqua-colored dress with a coral band across one shoulder. Even to someone as fashion-challenged as him, the hues were a perfect complement to her warm Caribbean island-girl skin.

Fee stepped away from him and walked over to her friend, taking both her hands as they each gave the other a critical once-over.

"Love that color on you," Lulu said.

"Ditto. Your makeup is fantastic."

Clint had to smile at their mutual admiration society, appreciating how easily they communicated, how in tune they seemed to be. This was friendship, he realized. The give and take, the easy, genuine compliments. He didn't have a friend like hers, not anymore.

And whose fault was that? The vets who worked for him were his employees and he'd isolated himself after leaving the military, he'd brushed off offers of help, of company, the invitation to join the TCC. Fee had become his closest friend since leaving his unit and she'd be leaving soon and he'd go back to his solitary life.

Or maybe he didn't have to. Maybe, when she left, instead of brooding at home, he could invite some of the volunteer firefighters to Rockwell Ranch for a barbecue. He could join the TCC. He could start, slowly, to reintegrate himself into the community.

He'd need a distraction to keep him from missing Fee...

But, still...*people.*

He'd see. Fee needed to leave and then he'd reevaluate his life. Hell, for all he knew he might just slide back into being the crotchety bastard he'd been before Hurricane Fee blew into his life. That was definitely the easier option—interacting with people took work…

But sometimes, like with Fee, the result—laughter, a connection, frickin' great sex—was worth it.

Fee's hand on his arm jerked him back to the present. He looked at her gorgeous, puzzled face. Did he have shaving cream on his cheek, something in his teeth? "What?"

"You just zoned out there for a minute," Fee replied, linking her fingers with his. "Ready to face the good citizens of Royal?"

Her hand felt right in his. Escorting her to the TCC clubhouse felt like it was something he was meant to do. But he did know his presence would set the gossip chain on fire.

Anything for Fee…

He smiled at her before returning his attention to Lulu. "Would you like to join us, Lulu?"

Lulu was opening her mouth to reply when they heard footsteps approaching them and Kace LeBlanc turned the corner, stopping abruptly when he caught sight of Lulu. Yep, that was what stunned looked like.

LeBlanc recovered a lot quicker than Clint had.

"Ladies, you look lovely," Kace said, approaching them with his hand outstretched for Clint to shake. He greeted Kace and returned his hand to Fee's back.

"Are you going to ride with us, Lulu?" Fee asked.

"I can give her a ride," Kace offered. "I came to

collect Miranda but she's left already. I have space for you two as well, if you'd prefer not to take your car," Kace told Clint.

Clint considered it for a minute, thinking it would be nice to have a couple of beers and not have to worry about going over the limit. Then he shook his head. "I appreciate the offer but I'd prefer to have my own vehicle in case another fire sparks and I have to leave quickly."

Kace nodded. "Understood." He looked at Lulu. "Ms. Sheppard?"

Even Clint, socially inept as he was, heard the challenge in Kace's voice. He looked at Fee and raised his eyebrows, silently asking whether he was imagining the electricity arcing between the tall lawyer and Fee's gorgeous friend.

Fee winked at him and they waited for Lulu's answer. Lulu eventually lifted her chin and nodded, with all the condescension of a Nubian queen.

"Thank you. Are you driving or do you have a driver?" Lulu demanded.

Ooh, snooty.

"I have a driver. Sorry, but you'll have to tolerate my presence for a very short time," Kace smoothly replied. "Just as I will have to tolerate yours."

Clint pulled a face at Fee, who was trying not to laugh.

Lulu looked at Fee. "Have bail money ready in case I kill him on the short drive from the resort to the club."

Fee struggle to keep her face impassive. "Always. Remember, jail orange is not your color."

Lulu picked up the skirts of her floor-length dress and arched an imperious eyebrow at LeBlanc "Shall we go?"

"Yes, your highness."

That wasn't a compliment, Clint thought as Kace and Lulu walked down the passage ahead of them. When they were out of earshot, he turned to Fee, laughter bubbling in his chest. "What the hell was that?" he asked.

Fee giggled. "Aren't they too precious for words? All growly and snarly and irritated because they are both too stubborn to admit they desperately want to see the other naked."

"Kind of like us when we first met," Clint said.

"Exactly like us," Fee cheerfully stated as she tucked her hand into the crook of his elbow. "I hope they eventually have the same fabulous time we've had. But they are running out of time—we're leaving Royal soon."

Yeah, did she have to remind him?

Miranda entered the ballroom at the TCC clubhouse by herself, choosing to make the silent statement that she was fine on her own, that she didn't need the acceptance of Royal residents, the members of the Texas Cattleman's Club or her stepchildren.

Stepchildren who were closer to her age than she'd been to their father's. Stepchildren who'd resented her role in their father's life even before he'd left her the inheritance they thought should be theirs.

Dammit, Buck, my life was perfect before you dropped this mess in my lap.

Miranda took a glass of champagne from a tray and caught a glimpse of her reflection in one of the many mirrors in this ballroom. She was pleased with her tight silver dress; it showed off her fantastic cleavage and the embroidered pattern between her breasts and hips highlighted her curves. The slit that came halfway up her thigh revealed her toned leg.

She looked good.

Looking good was great armor.

"Miranda."

Miranda turned and sighed at Kellan Blackwood's tight face. He'd found love with Buck's housekeeper and she looked around to see if she could spot the woman who'd been a faithful friend to her and Buck, in spite of Kellan's anger and resentment toward them both.

Not seeing Irina, Miranda forced a smile, knowing many eyes were watching their exchange. The cameras were also pointed in her direction, and she knew when the viewers watched this episode of *Secret Lives*, they'd wait in eager anticipation for the fireworks.

But, unlike some of her costars, she didn't seek notoriety. "Let's not make a scene, Kellan. It's New Year's Eve and this is supposed to be a happy event."

"I'm not the one who came back to Royal, determined to cheat a family out of their home and their father's wealth. I'm not the one who brought a camera crew with her to document the process," Kellan said, keeping his voice low.

He made it sound like she had complete control over the directors and producers, just as he apparently thought she'd controlled Buck. Miranda felt a headache building between her eyes. "Yeah, that's exactly what I did, Kellan. Where's Irina?"

"She's talking to Sophie." Miranda looked across the room to where her stepdaughter stood, tall and curvy, her dark hair and olive complexion the exact opposite of the Irina's pale skin, blond hair and blue eyes. Night and day, sun and moon, Miranda thought. Not unlike the way one of them liked and trusted her while the other passionately detested her.

Kellan also loathed her. So why was he talking to her? Why he was confronting her in front of everyone? He had to know their interaction would cause tongues to wag. Not that she cared about what the good residents of Royal thought, but he should.

"Say what you want to say, Kellan, and let's move on," Miranda said, giving him a tight smile.

Kellan's hand tightened around the tumbler of whiskey in his hand. "Irina and I were married in Nashville."

Whoa. Okay, then. "Congratulations?" Miranda posed the word as a question.

"We're very happy," Kellan stated, sounded defensive.

"Okay?" Another one-word answer, framed as a question. She saw the irritation flash in his eyes and smiled. These Blackwood children deserved to feel a little of the irritation, and annoyance, she constantly lived with.

"I want to make it perfectly clear I'm still going to fight you, tooth and nail, to win back my father's estate. We will claw back everything he gave you, Miranda."

This. Again. God, she was so tired. Instead of replying, Miranda just waited him out, knowing he would fill the silence she created.

"My wife wants to make Royal our base."

"What about your businesses in Nashville?"

"I'll travel back and forth to Nashville, as needed," Kellan said. "I just wanted you to know marriage hasn't made me soft. I still intend to fight you for everything you took from my siblings and me."

Same old same old. Miranda opened her mouth to blast him then remembered where she was and that the guests and the cameras were waiting for her to blow. She wouldn't give either audience the pleasure. "Noted."

Kellan waited for her to say more and when she just sipped her champagne, his frown deepened. "Is that all you have to say?"

Miranda nodded. "For now."

"What the hell does that mean?" Kellan demanded.

Just because it would make good TV, and because it would confuse the hell out of him, his siblings and everyone watching, Miranda reached up and placed a kiss on his cheek. Making sure her voice carried to both the guests, the cameras and the roving microphone held by the *Secret Lives* sound guy, she smiled at him as she wiped her lipstick off his cheek with her thumb.

"Congratulations, darling. I hope you and Irina are very happy together, like I was with your father."

Miranda heard the collective intake of breath, the murmurs following her controversial statement. Then she walked away, thinking the world couldn't prove or disprove her statement. Despite their divorce, nobody had known the true state of her marriage to Buck and she intended to keep it that way.

The cast of *Secret Lives* weren't the focus tonight and the cast wasn't miked so Fee didn't have to watch what she said. They'd been told the coverage of the ball would be minimal and they only needed to make a few direct-to-camera comments apiece and they'd be done.

And that meant Fee could have a quiet conversation with her best friend, who was, she reluctantly admitted, looking a little shell-shocked.

Leaving Clint talking to James Harrison, the TCC president—Clint being present at this party was causing a stir and everybody wanted a word with him—Fee walked over to where Lulu was standing on her own by a potted plant, looking a little dazed and a lot confused.

Fee walked up to her, put her arm around her friend's waist and gently turned her so they were both angled toward the wall and the room couldn't watch their interaction.

"Sweetie, are you okay?"

Lulu's lovely eyes met Fee's as she lifted a hand to her mouth and shook her head. "Not really."

Fee heard the panic in Lu's voice and instinctively went into mama-bear mode. Something was wrong and she was going to kick some lawyer's ass. She didn't think that Kace LeBlanc had hurt Lulu, she couldn't imagine him doing that. But something had happened…and she might have to get her ex-army ranger boyfriend—lover, fling, whatever—to knock him all the way across Texas.

"If said something that really hurt you, I will rip him apart," Fee muttered. "What did he say to you?"

Lulu shook her head and held up her hands. "Nothing."

Fee narrowed her eyes. "Then why are you looking all dazed and freaked out and crazy?"

Lulu placed her hand on her heart and gnawed on her inside of her cheek. "Because it was so damn fantastic, Fee. How can someone I loathe make me feel so…spacey?"

Okay, time to play catch-up. "What, exactly, happened on your five-minute drive, Miss Lulu?"

"Fastest, sexiest, craziest five minutes of my life," Lulu told her, pink in her cheeks.

"I swear, Lu, if you don't spill, I'm going to beat it out of you."

Lulu sighed and sighed again. "We didn't speak, at all, from the time we left you until we reached the limo waiting under the portico of The Bellamy. He opened the back door for me, I got in and he sat opposite me. The driver pulled off, Kace looked at me and…bam!"

Bam? What did that mean?

"I'm not sure whether he moved first or I did, but our eyes just connected and the next minute my dress was up around my waist and I was straddling his thighs and his hands were on my butt and his tongue was in my mouth and… *God.*"

Whoa. Hot damn.

"Not one word, we just kissed and kissed and…" Lulu saw a waiter carrying a tray of champagne and snapped her fingers to grab his attention. Lulu picked a glass up from the tray and downed the contents. She snagged the waiter's arm before he could walk away, handing Fee a glass before gulping a second one herself.

Fee stopped her from reaching for a third. "Nope, no throwing more liquor down your throat. Tell me what happened next."

The waiter finally escaped and Lu held her empty glass to her chest. "The limo stopped. Kace—" he was Kace now, Fee noticed, not Mr. Stick-Up-His-Ass as Lu normally called him "—put me back on the seat. He climbed out of the car, looking super cool, and helped me out. He walked me into the ballroom in complete silence, handed me a glass of champagne and a sarcastic smile and then walked away without looking back. I've been in a daze ever since."

Interesting. Lulu wasn't the type to lose her head over a man. "Wow. Just…wow."

Lulu frowned. "How can someone who irritates me

so intensely set my panties alight? Fee…" She held her index finger and thumb an inch apart. "I was this close to letting him nail me in the back of the limo. It's stupid, and silly, and annoying and incomprehensible."

"It's chemistry."

"Or I have multiple personalities and the crazy woman inside me is making her presence known," Lulu muttered. "Maybe I'm simply psychotic."

"Chemistry," Fee insisted.

"I'd prefer to be psychotic," Lulu retorted. She tossed back her hair, straightened her spine and lifted her chin. Yep, Queen Lulu was back. "I will not let him affect me. I will not make a big deal about a hot kiss from a man who doesn't like me enough to try and make conversation. I deserve to be treated better."

"You do," Fee said. Then she looked past her friend to see Kace watching Lulu with all the intensity of a Category 10 storm. He looked as flustered as Lu had earlier.

Yeah, she didn't think Kace was as unaffected as Lulu assumed.

Oh, this was going to be fun to watch.

"He's looking at you," Fee told her and Lu jerked her head around to scan the room. Kace had turned his attention back to the group of men surrounding him but his smirk told Fee he was very aware Lu's eyes were on him.

"This is so high school," Lu muttered, closing her eyes.

Nope, unlike Fee's experiences of high school, this was *fun*.

Eight

Sophie Blackwood stood between her two brothers, dwarfed as she always was by their height and good looks. It had always been the three of them and she was the baby, protected and, she guessed, cosseted. But now Kellan had his arm around the very beautiful Irina. While Sophie liked her brand-new sister-in-law, she felt like everything was changing too quickly and their lives were spinning out of control.

She wanted her dad to be alive, to be able to call Blackwood Hollow home again, to not have to fight Miranda Blackwood for what should be legally theirs. What the hell had their father been thinking leaving everything to Miranda and nothing to them? Had he really hated them that much?

Sophie looked across the room and watched the

redheaded woman flirting with someone whose name she couldn't recall but whom she recognized as being a past president of the TCC. The man looked like his tongue was about to fall on the floor at her feet.

Miranda was a beautiful woman and beautiful women had always been her father's weakness. She'd been aware of his affairs from a young age, had met many potential stepmothers but Miranda, thirty years younger than Buck, was the one he'd married minutes after the ink on his divorce papers to Sophie's mom were signed.

Buck had moved on from his wife quickly and it seemed, by leaving everything to Miranda, he'd moved on from his kids as well. His relationship with all of them had been distant at best—problematic at worst—but she'd always thought they'd have a chance to resolve things. That chance was gone now. God, it hurt.

Sophie felt Vaughn's hand on her back and she looked at her brother, gorgeous with blue eyes and his sharp-enough-to-cut-glass jaw. She saw the worry on his face and tried to give him a reassuring smile.

When Vaughn asked her if she was okay, she knew he wasn't fooled.

Sophie shrugged. "As well as can be expected." She tapped her fingernail against the glass of her flute and frowned. "I'm so angry at him, Vaughn. And at her."

Vaughn knew exactly to whom she was referring.

"I know, kiddo. We all are. And now we have to deal with meeting, at some point, a half-brother. Jesus."

He looked at Kellan and Irina, who were exchanging a long, loving look. Sophie rolled her eyes at Vaughn. "At least something good has come out of this mess."

"Yeah, they look happy."

Kellan turned his attention to them. "We are happy."

"Very happy," Irina said, laying her head on his shoulder.

Sophie, never having experienced love like that, tried to control her jealousy. How amazing would it be to feel so at ease with someone, to find the one person you clicked with? She was happy for Kell, she really was, even if she wasn't happy about not being at their wedding.

"I cannot believe you got married on the sly," Sophie stated.

Kellan sighed. "Here we go again."

Sophie ignored him and looked at Irina. "Didn't you want the pretty dress and the vows said in front of a pastor?" Sophie demanded. "The presents and the first dance?"

"I just wanted Kellan," Irina said simply. "The rest is just icing on the cake."

"Icing on the wedding cake you never got to eat," Sophie muttered.

Vaughn laughed. "Give it up, Soph."

Sophie saw Kellan look across to Miranda and his eyes hardened. "I told her we were married and our fight is far from over."

"Good for you," Sophie replied. "Did you also tell her we think she's a classless, over-exercised fortune hunter and that we will wrest her grubby hands off Dad's assets if it's the last thing we do?"

Vaughn smiled at her bloodthirstiness but gestured to draw Sophie's attention toward Irina, who looked uncomfortable. "Easy there, tiger."

Irina excused herself to go to the ladies' room, and Sophie released a huff of exasperation. "I didn't mean to upset Irina—I just get so frustrated with this whole mess! The inheritance, the fact that we have a half-brother out there somewhere. I need answers to how this all happened. But we've only run into dead ends in Royal."

Kellan placed his hands on her shoulders and squeezed. "I understand your frustration, Soph, I'm equally pissed off. But, to be honest, I'm not sure how to unravel this mess."

"I could go to New York City and see if I could dig up some dirt on Miranda."

"And how would you do that, Soph? You're not exactly a PI," Vaughn scoffed.

"I have another idea," Sophie said, choosing her words carefully. "I've been researching reality show TV and I know they film everything and they have hours and hours of outtakes stored…somewhere. I'm pretty sure there will be some compromising footage somewhere. I just need a plan to get it," Sophie mused. "But I'll have to go to New York, I can't do anything from here."

"I don't think that's such a good idea," Kellan responded.

"Why not?" Sophie demanded.

"It's New York, Soph." Vaughn immediately sided with Kellan, both going into protective mode.

"And I'm twenty-seven years old, not a child," Sophie replied, her tone heated. "I need to do something, guys. I can't just sit on my hands, hoping something will change."

Vaughn rubbed the back of his neck. "I don't like it, Sophie."

"Me neither."

"You don't have to like it," Sophie informed them, her determination only growing in the face of their resistance. "I'm an adult and if I want to go to New York, or any other city, I can. If I want to try and track down some footage, that's my prerogative. All you can do is support me. And say thank you when I find something."

When, not if. She refused to accept any other option.

Clearly realizing that she wouldn't back down, Kellan sighed and gave in, shoulders slumping with resignation. "Don't do anything stupid or illegal, Soph. And if you find yourself out of your depth, you come home."

Sophie rolled her eyes at his comment but she knew when to retreat, when to quit when she was ahead. "I'm a Blackwood," she reminded her brothers. "I'll do whatever is necessary—nothing more...and nothing less."

* * *

Fee loved her Bellamy hotel suite, from the bright purple door to the spacious hallway, the cool tones of the lavender-and-white color scheme and the natural light. She loved the French doors and high ceilings but she still would prefer to be on Rockwell Ranch, in Clint's gray-and-black bedroom, rolling around on his sheets.

Having sex in a hotel room brought home the impermanence of their relationship, made what they had feel more like a hookup and a fling...

But it *was* a hookup and a fling, wasn't it?

Fee kicked off her heels in the luxurious sitting area and switched on a lamp. She was leaving soon, leaving Royal and leaving him, and if she was thinking this could be more, that they could have more, she was setting herself up for a hard fall.

She would move on; it was what she did. Always.

She couldn't forget that.

Fee watched Clint shed his jacket and silently admitted a part of her loved the fantasy of being Clint's, of being one half of a whole. They'd had a magical evening and Clint, despite his loner personality, had seemed to enjoy himself, even slow dancing with her to one of her favorite songs. Despite the avid interest of the other guests, he'd kissed her—a kiss that was far too heated and went on for far too long for propriety—when the old year flipped over into the new.

The society columns and entertainment sites would be buzzing with speculation.

She hadn't cared then and she didn't care now. She was with Clint and that was all that mattered.

"Fun evening," Clint said, loosening his bow tie and flipping open the button holding his collar together. He looked around, saw the crystal decanters on a bar set up in the corner and his long strides covered the distance in a few steps. "Would you like a nightcap?"

"Cointreau, thanks," Fee answered him, sinking into the corner of the sofa and tucking her feet under her.

Clint handed her a drink and sat down next to her, pulling her legs over his thighs. He held her ankle as he sipped his drink.

"Happy New Year, Fee."

Fee smiled. "You too, Clint. I hope this year brings you so much happiness."

She wouldn't be around to witness what direction his life would take but she hoped he wouldn't retreat back into his lonely world—she hoped he'd make an effort to be more sociable. She could tell he'd had fun tonight; he'd enjoyed the company of his fellow ranchers, of the businesspeople in Royal, his town.

It wasn't hers. She'd like it to be but she wasn't the type to settle down, and she didn't think she could live in a small town where everyone knew each other's business, where you couldn't sneeze without someone across town sending a *bless you* your way. She'd hate it, she'd feel confined and hemmed in and claustrophobic…

But Clint was here and he made her feel free, accepted, protected.

What was the point in even considering it, though? Even if she could wrap her head around staying in one place—a massive "if"—Clint had never, not once, hinted he'd like her to stay. She was just a fling, someone to share a little of the holiday season with, some fun in the middle of a harsh winter.

Even if she wanted to, it wouldn't be fair to change the rules of the game on him now.

Fee rested her head on the back of the sofa and sighed, enjoying the way Clint's thumbs pressed into pressure points in her foot. She moaned, feeling heat slide into her veins and sparkles dance across her skin. They'd made love often but she still felt a hit of anticipation. He made her feel new, precious, undiscovered.

Even, she thought, *a little loved.*

But love was out of the question, and not something either of them was looking for. So why was she feeling this way? "You're looking a little pensive," Clint commented, placing his glass on the coffee table in front of them.

"It's a fresh start, a new year. A perfect time to feel pensive," Fee replied. She took a sip of her liqueur, sighing when the warmth hit her stomach.

Clint lifted her legs off his and stood up. Bending down, he pushed one hand under her thighs, another around her back and lifted her, with no effort at all, into his arms.

She still had her drink in her hand.

"Where's your bedroom?" Clint demanded.

Fee waved her glass in the direction of the hall-way. "Last room on the right."

Clint carried her past the dining table and stepped into the dark hall while Fee continued to sip her drink, very confident in his ability to carry her. He kicked open her door and walked her across the lux-urious room to lay her in the middle of her enor-mous, too-big-for-one-person bed. Clint took her drink from her hand, threw the last sip of Cointreau down his throat and placed the glass on the bureau behind him.

"I can't think of a better way to start a new year, Martinez," Clint stated, his voice extra growly. "You, a splash of orange on that white bed, eyes dark and mysterious in the shadows. Take down your hair."

Fee blinked at the unexpected command but she lifted her hands, pulling the pins out of the compli-cated knot her stylist had created at the back of her head. She placed the hairpins on the bedside table and allowed her heavy mass of curls to fall over her shoulders, down her back.

"You are so beautiful, Seraphina. I'm always going to remember this night."

She would too. She would remember him stand-ing in front of her bay windows, moonlight high-lighting the blond in his hair, turning his eyes from green to gold.

She'd remember the way his white shirt caressed those broad shoulders, how well he wore his tuxedo.

"I don't want this to end, Clint," Fee admitted,

bending her legs and wrapping her arms around her knees.

"I know. I don't either," Clint said, coming to sit beside her on the bed, his fingers sliding into her hair. "But it has to end, sweetheart, because neither of us can change."

She could, maybe, if she tried hard enough. Clint shook his head when she suggested it.

"You're a beautiful butterfly who needs to experience the taste of different places and I need to be here, in Royal. Neither of us can—should—change."

His words hurt but the truth always did. "I know." Fee pushed her cheek into his palm, turning her head to kiss his calloused skin. "I just can't imagine not doing this again."

Clint held her cheek, his eyes a soft green-gold. "We've just got to enjoy the time we have and make some great memories."

He was right, they couldn't waste a second. Life was too short and their remaining time was minimal. Fee placed her hand on his knee, feeling the outline of his prosthetic under her fingers. Clint looked down and smiled. "You make me feel whole, Fee, normal."

Fee placed a gentle kiss on his lips. "You are whole, and you're better than normal—you're extraordinary."

Clint held her face and gently kissed her lips, in a caress that was as magical as it was erotic. "I want to make this last," he murmured against her lips, "I want to savor, to commit every caress to memory."

While that sounded wonderful, Fee knew herself all too well. "I'm not very patient, Clint."

"Suck it up, cupcake." Clint smiled against her mouth. Tipping her face, he changed the angle of his kiss and slid his tongue into her mouth, tangling with hers in a languid exchange that seemed to last for days, years.

Fee leaned back against the pillows and Clint covered her body with his as they kissed, fully dressed. This wasn't just sex; he was making love to her and Fee's heart expanded to explosion point.

She would take this night, and the memory, and thank God that, at least once, she'd known true passion.

Clint undressed her slowly, sliding her dress off her body and dropping the magnificent garment to the floor. She lay on the bed in her tiny flame-colored thong and gold spiked heels, her body flushed with pleasure. Clint stroked her from neck to foot, committing every curve, bump and freckle to memory. Fee tried to touch him in return but he moved her hands back to her sides, telling her this was his time to feast.

He loved her breasts, pulling her nipple between his teeth, easing the sting with his tongue. He buried his nose into her belly button, gently nipped her hip. He kissed the back of her knees, nibbled her ankle just below the strap of her heels.

Somewhere along the way he shed his clothes and allowed her to use her hands, her mouth, to torture him as he had her.

By the time she'd finished paying his body the

same attention he'd paid hers, they were both vibrating with need, desperate to fly. Clint settled himself between her legs and rested his weight on his elbows next to her head. "Fee, look at me."

Fee lifted her heavy lids, sighing when he slid into her, hard and masculine, filling her, completing her.

"Remember this night…when you feel lonely or less than or sad, remember this night, remember me. Remember that I was profoundly, deeply grateful to share this with you. Remember that I think you are amazing and how your beauty makes my heart stutter. Remember this, remember me," Clint said, placing a hand under her butt to lift her up and into him.

Fee held his face as he rocked her up, and up. "I will. I always will. Will you remember too?"

Clint nodded, his eyes foggy with desire, his back tense from holding back. "I'll never forget you, Fee."

Fee smiled, nodded and closed her eyes as she followed him over the edge.

Nine

On the first day of the New Year, Fee, curled up against Clint's broad back, heard the beep of an incoming message on her phone and released a long groan. She gently banged her head against Clint's spine before rolling away from him to scoop her phone up off the bedside table. Pushing her hair out of her face, she squinted at the screen and cursed.

"Such ladylike language on the first day of the New Year," Clint teased, slinging a leg over her thigh and covering her breast with his big hand.

Fee dropped the phone onto the mattress and rolled her head to look into his pretty eyes. "We need to do some filming today, and I really don't want to. I'd rather spend the day in bed with you."

Clint lifted his wrist to look at his watch. "It's barely six. What time do you need to report for duty?"

"Ten."

"I need to get back to the ranch." He dropped his mouth to her shoulder, nuzzling his cheek against her skin. "Do you want to come with me? I can check on my guys, the animals and I'll feed you breakfast. I'll have you back in town by ten."

She couldn't think of anything she'd like to do more. "Yes, please." She sighed as she rolled onto her side. "I'd much rather spend the day with you than filming."

"I don't know how you cope with having those cameras in your face all the time."

"You get used to it."

"It would be my worst nightmare." Clint stroked her arm from shoulder to elbow, his touch light and soothing. "Do you enjoy it?"

"Enjoy what?"

"Being a reality TV star? Having to look good all the time, being careful what you say and how you say it?"

Fee thought for a moment. Before she came to Royal, she would've quickly responded she loved it, that going to work every day was fun. And in many ways, it was—she'd had a lot of experiences she never could have had without the show opening doors for her, as she explained to Clint.

"I've traveled, a lot, seen places that would've been out of my budget on a normal salary. I've earned a lot of money over the years. Money that will allow me to keep traveling, to keep being able to see new places, do new things. To keep moving."

"And that's important to you, being on the move?"

Was it? She was no longer so sure. "It's what I know, Clint. As a kid, we moved every six to eight to ten months. The longest we stayed in one town was just over a year." Fee sat up and pulled the sheet over her breasts. "I like being with people, probably because I spent so much of my childhood and teenage years on my own. The show, the people working on it, are my family."

"But you will lose them if you leave the show and move on."

And that was something that still worried her... They'd been such a part of her life for so long. Could she could cope without being part of a group, not having people around her 24/7? Yeah, she thought she'd be okay. She'd miss her friends, miss the crew and the constant company, but she wouldn't be completely lost without them.

"Being here in Royal, learning the basics of ranching—"

Clint snorted. "Please. You didn't even scratch the surface of what it means to ranch..."

"Okay, point taken, we didn't take it very seriously."

"Or at all," Clint muttered.

Fee ignored his interruption. "But I would've like to have learned more. It's an interesting process. And I think I could be good at it."

"Mucking out a horse stall and counting cattle doesn't make you a rancher, Fee."

"I know that. I just said it's interesting. I like being in the fresh air, doing something with my hands, seeing immediate results. It's…life-affirming, I suppose." Fee looked through the open drapes at the day starting to unfurl outside. "I like the animals, the big sky, feeling grounded."

"Careful, you're starting to sound a little in love with Royal, with the ranching lifestyle," Clint teased.

That might be because Fee *had* fallen a little in love with Royal, with the town and the land and the relaxed lifestyle. And she was, terrifyingly, more than a little in love with Clint. Fee nibbled on the inside of her lip as she watched the sun's weak rays touch the huge lake she could see from her bed.

When had that happened? She couldn't tell; it had slowly crept up on her. Maybe it was his refusal to be pigeonholed by his disability. Maybe it was because he was strong and decisive and a natural leader. His super-fine body played one part and his skill as a lover another. Under his taciturn exterior was a guy who just wanted the world to see him for what he was and not how he looked.

The residents of Royal did see him for what he was—it was only Clint who thought they were judging him by his disability.

They admired him and Clint still couldn't see it. He was still convinced they only saw the guy with the prosthetic. That was why he pushed himself so hard, why he was determined to fund the fire station, to act as their temporary Fire Chief. He wanted the world to see he was more than a guy who'd lost half his leg.

Fee could relate. She wanted the world to know she was more than a pretty face, a party animal, the high-spirited, loud-mouthed, fast-talking delight she was shown as on TV. Up until her visit to Royal she'd been content with the way the world saw her but after a few short weeks in this town, she understood, on a fundamental level, Clint's need to be recognized for who he was and not what he looked like.

She got it, she really did. Because the world didn't see her clearly either.

So was she confusing love with understanding, blowing their mutual connection out of proportion? She'd never been in love before so she wasn't sure, but it was something to think about. She also needed to give some thought to her future, to what she did next. But she'd need to leave Royal to do that. She needed to see if she still felt this way when she was back in New York, back in her apartment.

Back in Manhattan, she'd be able to think clearly again.

Turning back to Clint, she saw his eyes were closed and his breathing had evened out. His eyelashes were long on his cheeks and she could see hints of gold in his stubble. In sleep his lips were relaxed, his hair messy. Fee pulled back the sheet and looked down at the hard muscles of his stomach, his early morning erection, her eyes wandering down his thighs, over his knee and to his long, elegant foot.

His prosthetic was propped up against the bedside table and she was so thankful he had the money to pay for one of the most advanced systems in the world. She had no doubt Clint would've gotten by on a cheaper version, or on crutches, but his variety of robotic legs gave him amazing freedom of movement.

"You're thinking too loud," Clint muttered, kissing her shoulder again.

"I thought you were asleep," Fee replied.

"Dozing," Clint said, sitting up. He kneeled and, gripping her under her thighs, pulled her down the bed. Then he rolled on top of her, his cock settling within the V of her legs.

Fee lifted her eyebrows, instantly aroused. "I thought we didn't have time."

"We don't but I need you. I need to have you again."

Fee turned into his embrace and sighed when Clint kissed her.

Best way to start a New Year, bar none.

Clint heard the twang of a country song coming from the speakers of his SUV and hit the button on his steering wheel to mute the music. He smiled when Fee hit the radio to bring the song up again so he flipped the station to a heavy rock channel. "It's too early in the morning for slit-my-throat music, sweetheart."

"It's country—you're a rancher and a Texan, you're supposed to like country music."

"I don't," Clint replied, lifting his take-out cup of coffee to his mouth.

"It tells a story, and it's moving."

"It's depressing," Clint said, amused. His city slicker was really throwing herself into country living. He looked at her outfit and shook his head. Okay, it wasn't quite so over-the-top country as her first cowgirl outfit, but her jeans were tucked into a brand-new pair of tooled brown cowboy boots and she wore a sleeveless navy padded vest over a long-sleeved, pale pink T-shirt. The voluminous scarf in greens and blues made her eyes seemed darker and edgier.

She was the sexiest cowgirl he'd ever met...

Clint sipped his coffee and thought about their evening spent in Royal. Despite his bitching about the camera crews and dressing up in the tux, he'd had fun the previous night. He'd met several new members of the Texas Cattleman's Club and he'd enjoyed talking ranching and oil and beef prices. Despite the wealth, the glitz and the over-decorated ballroom, he'd felt more at home than he'd thought he would.

But the after-party in Fee's suite had been the highlight of the evening. He'd sipped champagne from her belly button, from the hollow of her back, trickled drops over her hard nipples. They'd loved and laughed and talked and loved and laughed and talked some more. He really wished they could spend the whole day on his ranch—saddle up two horses, go for a ride and, later, fall asleep, preferably naked, in the afternoon sun, hitting his bed in the middle of the afternoon.

He'd had little to no sleep and, God, he wasn't seventeen anymore. He needed to recharge…

"Clint?"

Something about Fee's voice jerked his attention back and he looked at her, frowning. "What is it?"

"Smoke."

The single word hit him with all the force of a bullet and Clint pulled his foot off the accelerator and looked toward where she was pointing. A massive black cloud hovered over the ridge and he cursed. That wasn't good, not at all.

Clint pulled over and reached for his cell phone. As he picked up the device to make a call, it rang. He swiped the screen to answer. "Jeff, yeah, I see the smoke. Blackwood Hollow?"

Jeff, one of his more experienced volunteers and the guy he wanted to be appointed as Royal's first permanent fire chief, didn't waste time with explanations. "The fire was started by kids smoking at the reservoir."

The reservoir was in a secluded area to the north of town where teenagers frequently met to party and let off steam. Clint cursed.

Jeff ignored him and continued. "These dry and windy conditions aren't helping. The fire is moving rapidly towards Blackwood Hollow. There are also fires north of Royal, and there's another one heading towards the TCC clubhouse."

Clint ignored Fee's big eyes and her inquisitive expression. He rapidly accelerated. "I'm heading toward Blackwood Hollow. When can I expect help?"

"Twenty minutes, maybe thirty?" Jeff replied.

"Tell them to hurry the hell up," Clint told him. He barked out another list of instructions, including a request for surrounding counties to send their people in to help. It was a crap start to the New Year but they'd have to deal.

And get the damn fire under control.

Clint cut his call to Jeff, made a few more calls and handed his phone to Fee. Keeping an eye on the column of smoke, which was to his left and growing bigger, he whipped into the driveway of Blackwood Hollow. He looked at the wind causing the trees to sway and felt dread curl in his stomach. The direction of the wind would push the fire directly toward Blackwood Hollow, and the house, stables and barn would be in its fiery path in no time at all.

"Is Rockwell Ranch safe?"

"Right now it is," Clint tersely replied. "The wind is sending the fire this direction, not toward my spread. But if the wind changes, everything could change."

"Don't you need to be there?" Fee asked, her hand on the dashboard in front of her.

"I spoke to my foreman. Brad has it under control. We go where the biggest threat is."

"Understood. What's the plan?"

"The plan is that you go into the underground bunker and stay put."

Fee's hard "No" shot out of her mouth. "That's not going to happen."

"Jesus, Fee, I can't be effective while worrying about you."

"Understood," Fee replied. "And I will get in the bunker when there's nothing more I can do, when I'm getting in the way. But there must be something I can help with now. I'll go mad sitting on my ass in a bunker."

Fair point. She could help, and it wasn't unsafe for her yet. Clint thought for a moment as he drove past the house toward the stables. He jerked to a stop and released his seat belt. "Okay, it's early so the horses should still be in the barn. We're going to get them out."

"And take them where?" Fee asked, following him out of the car. She unwrapped her scarf and threw it, and her vest, onto the passenger seat.

"We'll take them into the north pasture for starters. Then I'll take the dirt bike and open a few gates and get them out of the paddocks and onto the range. Their instinct will take them away from the fire, to safety. We've just got to get them onto the open land and they'll head, hopefully, in the direction of Rockwell Ranch."

Clint saw the Blackwood hands pouring out of the bunkhouse and gestured them toward the other barn where all the working horses were stabled.

Clint headed to the second, smaller barn and Fee had to jog to keep up with his long legs. But he couldn't slow down, time was of the essence.

Clint headed into the first stall and ran his hand down the already sweaty neck of Buck's favorite stallion, Jack. "You can smell the smoke, can't you boy?" Clint kept his voice steady. "I need you to take your mares to safety. You can do that, can't you, Jack?"

Clint looked behind him to see Fee with her hands full of bridles. "Good thinking, sweetheart."

He quickly placed one over Jack's massive head and when he was done, handed the reins to Fee. "Lead him outside—do not let him bolt."

Fee took the reins and nodded, her eyes filled with fear. The horse was enormous next to her but Clint didn't have a choice, he needed to put bridles on the other ten horses.

His phone jangled and he pulled it out of his back pocket and didn't bother to greet Jeff again. "Yeah?"

"The intensity of the fire is building and it's quickly spreading. We need helicopters in the air, we need water dumps urgently. Blackwood Hollow is in immediate danger, Clint."

Clint ran over to the open door of the stable and saw the fire was so much closer than he'd believed. Smoke stung his eyes and he tasted the heat in the back of his throat. They were out of time. Cursing, he retraced his steps and flipped open the latches to all the stalls.

"Unhook Jack's reins and slap his rump, tell him to go," Clint yelled at Fee. "And stay out of the damn way!"

He poked his head out of the stall, saw Fee following his directions. The horse bolted. Fee waited until the huge horse passed her and ducked into the stall opposite. A heartbeat later, another horse, this time a black filly, galloped out. Within minutes they managed to clear the stable. Clint grabbed Fee's hand and they ran out of the building. Clint watched as Jack led his mares away from the fire, all of them easily clearing the low white fences.

Yeah, they'd be fine.

They moved to the other stable block and helped the hands release the rest of the stock. In minutes the barn was finally cleared of animals but the air was getting thicker, smokier by the minute. They needed to burn a firebreak to keep the fire from hitting the house but he also needed to be up in the air. He was one of the few helicopter pilots in the area and before donating a few birds to the town of Royal, he'd made sure his certification was current.

Clint grabbed Fee's hand, heard her cough and knew she needed to get underground as soon as possible. The hands would start burning a firebreak but there was still a damn good chance that Blackwood Hollow would be burned to the ground.

"Are there any people or animals in the main house?" Fee asked, after coughing.

Clint thought for a minute. "Miranda? She's living here now, isn't she?"

Fee nodded.

"Can you call her, get her out here? Then both of you can go into the bunker."

Fee shook her head. "I left my phone in the car. I'll just run over to the house and get her out."

Clint saw a convoy of cars speeding up the long driveway and nodded. Thank God, help had arrived.

"You have ten minutes. I'm serious, Fee, ten minutes to get her out. Meet me by the front door."

Fee nodded and turned to sprint toward the main house. Clint fought the urge to run after her, to keep her at his side, and told himself she was running away from the fire, that he needed her to get Miranda out. She'd be fine, there was no need to worry.

Kellan Blackwood was the first person to exit a vehicle, closely followed by his brother, Vaughn, and Clint nodded, grateful. Despite having been estranged from Buck, they were, at heart, ranch boys who loved this land. They had an added incentive to save Blackwood Hollow. Gage, Buck's foreman, who'd spent the night in town with his honey, hopped out of the second vehicle and Clint sent up another prayer.

Gage was old school, had fought the massive fire of eighty-two and knew exactly what to do.

Running over to them, Clint spoke directly to Gage. "You're in charge. Burn a break, slow the fire down. If you can't fight it, get everybody to the bunker, make sure your people are safe. Human life is what's important, buildings are not."

"Got it." Gage nodded. "We need a bird up in the air."

"I'm on that. Jeff let me know he's got a pilot out of Deer Springs to fly the other chopper."

Gage nodded. "That'll work. Right, let's beat this bastard."

Okay, they had a plan. Clint raised his hands at the other volunteer firefighters as he jogged to his vehicle but didn't stop to talk. There was no time. He needed to get Fee and Miranda into the bunker; she would be safe in the shelter Buck built to protect his people from tornadoes, storms and the end of the world, and Clint could do his job not worrying about his woman.

His woman...

Well, for now, today, she was.

Clint whipped his car around, punched the accelerator and drove up to the main house. He exited his SUV as the front door opened and he jogged up the steps to see Fee's white face. "She's not here. She must've stayed at The Bellamy last night."

"You sure?" Clint demanded, wondering whether he could spare the time to search the house himself.

Fee's look was sour. "I can search a house, Rockwell, even one as ridiculously big as this."

Point taken. "I trust you. Let's go."

Fee followed him into the kitchen and then down the stairs that led to a basement converted into a games room. Ignoring the massive TV and the billiards table, Clint headed for the far corner and twisted the painting to a forty-degree angle. Like magic, the wall slid away to reveal a steel door, complete with a brightly lit keypad. Clint punched in some numbers and light filled the room beyond the door.

"The code boots up the generator and filters the air coming into this safe room," Clint told her, gesturing her to step inside. It was a hell of a room, Clint thought. Couches, chairs and bookshelves filled the space. Bunk beds lined the far end of the room and, in the room adjoining this area were more bunks and a double bed.

If he didn't have a raging wildfire to fight, he could make good use of that bed.

"There's a shower and toilet through the door and drinks and nonperishables in the cupboards. Help yourself."

Fee folded her arms across her chest and looked apprehensive. Clint fought the urge to pull her into his arms, knowing he might not let her go. And he had to go.

"You'll be safe here, Fee. The fire, even if it takes the house, won't affect you. This room was built to hold twenty people, to keep them safe for three months or more. I promise you, you will be okay."

Fee rolled her eyes at him. "I'm not worried about me, you idiot, I'm worried about you. You're the one who's rushing into danger while I sit on my ass and do nothing."

Her obvious concern for his welfare touched his cold, shriveled heart. Clint clasped her face in his hands. "I'll be fine, sweetheart."

"Are you okay to fly the helicopter? You know, after having been in one that crashed?"

The crash was the reason he'd forced himself to learn to fly, getting back on the horse and all that…

"I've worked really hard to put that behind me, Fee."

"And you won't take any stupid risks just to prove you can?" Fee demanded. "I don't need a hero, Rockwell, I need you alive. To come back and get me."

"I won't be a hero." He'd do what he needed to do but he wouldn't take any unnecessary risks. Or he'd try not to. "And I've told Gage and the Blackwood boys, Kellan and Vaughn, you are in here. There's also a camera system for you to see whether the coast is clear. You can leave when you feel it's safe. I'd prefer for you to wait for me, though, so I'm asking you to wait for me to come and get you, Seraphina."

Fee nodded and Clint sighed at the tears in her eyes. "I'll be fine, Fee."

Fee smiled and knuckled the moisture away. "Of course, you will be. I, on the other hand, will be going crazy down here."

Clint kissed her nose.

Fee lifted herself up onto her tiptoes and brushed her lips across his. "Go now. Come back to me as soon as you can."

"That's a promise," Clint said, before dropping an open-mouthed kiss on her mouth. Allowing himself one last, quick taste, he pulled away and, without looking back, walked out of the safe room.

While he still could.

Ten

Fee stared at the TV screen, the image split into quarters, and wondered why she bothered. Twelve hours had passed since Clint pushed her into this underground bunker and night had long since fallen over Blackwood Hollow. Earlier, via the screen, she'd watched the fire reach the far barn, enveloping the structure in silky, almost pretty flames. The volunteers had allowed the structure to burn, choosing to put their efforts toward saving the newer stable block. She thought they might have succeeded, since the camera within that stable was still working while the other wasn't.

Fee folded her arms and looked at the solidly black screen. At least she couldn't see any more flames, and were those raindrops she saw on the lens of another camera?

God, she hoped so. It was time Mother Nature started working with them instead of against them.

Fee sat on the edge of one of the super-comfortable couches and held her shaking hands between her knees, trying not to cry. Was Clint safe? Where was he? Was he still flying, fighting fires? She knew some helicopter pilots were night rated and wondered if he was too. She was in awe of his bravery and determination. If she'd been in a crash, and if said crash had killed a few of her teammates, she doubted she'd go anywhere near a helicopter, or a plane, again. Hell, she'd have trouble with anything more than two feet off the ground.

But not Clint. Clint had looked at himself, realized he was scared and instead of retreating—like a normal person would—rushed headfirst into resolving his problem. He was scared so he needed to conquer his fear by learning to fly the damned machine, exerting his control over the situation.

He was pretty damn amazing and a real inspiration and, yep, she was very definitely in love with her superhero cowboy.

Dammit.

But any woman would be. He was sexy, sure, good looking, sure, and possessed awesome bed skills. But he was also intelligent, hardworking, determined and reliable. He gave and gave and gave and all he wanted was for people to see him as capable. He didn't want medals, recognition or kudos, he just wanted people to see him, not his disability.

And they did. Clint just had to recognize that truth.

Fee stared down at the concrete floor, trying not to look at her watch again. Not ten minutes had passed since she last checked the time, and God knew, a watched clock didn't move any faster. She'd tried to read, she'd tried to sleep, but nothing kept her occupied for long.

She'd mostly just spent the past twelve hours pacing the floor, worrying.

Should she open the bunker? Was she safe? She didn't know, but man, she needed to get out of here in the worst way. She needed to find Clint, to see if he was okay, to assess the damage done to this ranch, to Rockwell Ranch, to Royal itself. This might, after all, be her forever town.

But she didn't know what awaited her outside. The fire could still be raging off camera; she might be walking into hell itself. It was dark, and she didn't have transport.

She was, dammit, safe here. Safe and, since she couldn't find a phone or a radio, disconnected.

Fee tasted panic and forced it down. She'd fought occasional bouts of claustrophobia all afternoon and it had taken all she had not to wrench the door open and run out of the room.

But she wasn't a fool. She was safe here and she'd promised Clint to stay put.

He trusted her to keep her word, so she'd spend the night here, if necessary, and in the morning, she'd reassess the situation.

That meant spending more time in this box but she would deal…

Mostly because she didn't have a damn choice.

"Suck it up, cupcake." She repeated Clint's words and immediately felt steadier. Standing up, she walked into the bathroom and stared at her white face in the small mirror above the sink. There was nothing of Seraphina Martinez, reality TV star, in the mirror. She looked haggard, older, stressed.

Her man had been in danger all day; she had a right to look like crap. Fee splashed some water on her face and bent down to sip some out of her cupped hand. It slid down her tight throat and she felt a burning sensation in her eyes.

"You are not going to cry, dammit."

Fee headed into the main room, thinking of a way to distract herself. Maybe if she pushed the couch to the side, she could do some yoga, find her Zen.

Well, she could try.

Fee bent down, put her shoulder to the heavy couch and pushed, relieved when the couch scraped, reluctantly, across the smooth concrete. There still wasn't enough space so she pushed it again, totally surprised when the couch easily glided across the floor this time.

Lifting her head, she saw his yellow trousers, his bare arm, and she squealed when she saw his sooty face, his white teeth flashing. Launching herself up, she gave him just enough time to straighten from his bent position before throwing herself into his arms, gripping his waist with her legs and raining kisses on his filthy face.

"Oh, God, you're here. You're safe."

"I'm safe." Clint pushed his hand into her hair and held the back of her head. "How are you? Doing okay?"

"Pfft." Fee waved his concern away. "I'm fine. Bored but fine. What's the damage? Is your ranch okay?"

"The fire touched some land bordering my ranch but we got lucky. It started to rain and stopped it from spreading."

"It's really raining?"

"Bucketing down. Thank God," Clint replied. "It'll kill the last few sparks, the small fires."

"What about Blackwood Hollow? How much damage is there?" Fee demanded, sliding down his body and ignoring the streaks of dirt on her clothing.

"The far barn is gone, as is one of the stables. The guest house lost a couple of rooms." Clint pushed the braces off his shoulders and allowing his pants to slide down his legs. He kicked them away and stood in his jeans and T-shirt, looking exhausted but satisfied.

"Is Royal ok?" Fee asked as she headed toward the big fridge on the far side of the room. She pulled out a cola and popped the tab, handing it to Clint, who sat down on the edge of the bed, clearly exhausted.

"We lost a few houses on the edge of town, the TCC clubhouse has been damaged and there's smoke damage to a few businesses on the outskirts. There's a lot of work to do, clearing up and rebuilding."

"I learned how to wield a drill and a hammer when I worked on a Habitat for Humanity project last spring," Fee told him, sitting cross-legged on the bed beside him. "I can help."

"I'm sure we can use your skills." Clint drank deeply from the can and looked down at his black hands. "I'm filthy."

"I thought you were flying—not fighting the flames up close and personal."

"I was," Clint said, standing up. "Then I landed and another small blaze kicked up not far from where I was. It was quicker to beat the fire back toward the firebreak than fly the chopper to pick up another load of water."

Clint strolled into the bathroom and Fee heard the shower. "Let me clean up and then we'll head out to my place."

Fee thought for a minute and followed him into the bathroom. He cursed when he looked down at his leg. "Shit. I don't have any crutches here."

"Hang tight," Fee said. Without giving him chance to argue, she stripped off and bent down in front of Clint to remove his leg. She heard the pop of the suction cup and gently removed his prosthetic, resting it against the bathroom cabinet. Clint leaned against the wall and Fee placed her shoulder under his armpit, letting him lean on her while he hopped into the shower, adjusting the stream of water to hit him as he rested against the wall.

He reached for the soap and loofah but jerked his hand back to hold onto the edge of the shower door to keep his balance. "Crap, it's slippery in here."

Fee waited until she was sure he was balanced before leaving his side. She quickly stripped off her underwear and stepped into the shower. Grabbing the loofah, she dumped some liquid soap on it and started to wash Clint's body.

"Fee, I—"

Fee looked up at him, a frown on her face. "You've spent the past twelve hours helping your fellow ranchers, your fellow residents. You've fought fires, dumped water, flown a damned helicopter. You've helped and helped and served and served. Let me help you."

"I—"

"Just shut up, Rockwell," Fee told him, standing on her toes to drop a kiss on his mouth.

Not giving him more time to argue, she washed his shoulders, under his arms, across his chest and his stomach. She swiped the loofah over his private areas and down his leg, and then, equally clinically, over his short leg.

She took a washcloth, put soap on it and wiped his face. Seeing the dirty water streaming off his hair, she told him to duck his head. Picking up a bottle of shampoo, she washed his hair, once, then again.

"God, it feels so good to be clean," Clint told her, hot water pounding her head and his shoulders.

Fee wrinkled her nose. "Sorry, but you're going to have to get back into your dirty clothes."

Clint shook his head. "There's a cupboard full of clothes, different sizes and styles. I'll find something to wear."

"Buck really was prepared," Fee said, impressed.

"You have no idea." Clint wiped moisture off his face with his hand and switched off the water. "Let's get dressed and we can go home."

Fee saw the exhaustion in his red-rimmed eyes. She touched his cheek. "Do you have to go back? Is there something you need to do on the ranch tonight?"

"No, my foreman has it covered," Clint replied. "Why?"

"Because there's a very nice bed in the adjoining bedroom and I think we could both do with a some sleep."

"I thought you would be sick of this place by now, that you'd want to get out."

Fee handed him the truth. He was a big boy and she was sure he could handle it. "You're here now and I'm fine. Let's go to bed, Rockwell. I need to hold you and be held."

Clint nuzzled his cheek into her palm. "Me too, Fee. I need to hold you too. But I can only sleep for an hour, maybe two. There's so much I still need to get to tonight."

Because, if there was work to be done, Clint was first in line to do it. Fee loved that, and everything, about him.

Sophie Blackwood, dressed in her most ragged pair of jeans and oldest, most battered sweatshirt, picked her way through the debris of what was once the original stables housing the Blackwood family horses. These days, her father's prize horseflesh was stabled in the new climate controlled, technologically advanced stable block but she'd loved the history of the original stables.

It was gone now. Annihilated. Burned to the ground.

She shouldn't be this upset about it, Sophie admitted to herself, blinking away hot tears.

Everything was changing and she didn't like it.

Sophie felt a big hand on her back and turned to see Vaughn standing next to her, concern in his expression and in his eyes. "You okay, Soph?"

She wanted to be able to tell him she was fine but couldn't speak the lie. "The hits keep coming."

He rubbed a big circle on her back. "It could've been worse. The house could've burned down."

Sophie managed a weak smile. "This stable block meant more to me than the house. I never felt at home there." Sophie pushed back her deep-brown Stetson with her wrist. She bit her bottom lip. "We owe Clint Rockwell our gratitude, Vaughn. His quick response saved Blackwood Hollow, even if it's not ours anymore."

"I tried to thank him but he brushed me off," Vaughn said, looking over to where Rockwell stood. Kace and Lulu were standing just behind him, for once not arguing. Clint looked dead on his feet, pale with exhaustion. He'd gone above and beyond and Sophie, when the time was right, would express her gratitude, in her own way.

"Blackwood Hollow will be ours again," Vaughn assured her. "We just have to find a way."

"From your lips to God's ears," Sophie murmured. "Here comes Kell."

Sophie took one of the bottles of water Kellan held out, giving him a grateful smile. Cracking the lid, she heard the arrival of an expensive vehicle. Her oldest brother rolled his eyes and Sophie turned to see the Step Witch pulling off her designer sunglasses and exiting the expensive two-door coupe. Her hair was pulled back into a ponytail, her makeup was understated and she wore jeans and a long-sleeved, emerald silk T-shirt. Despite her attempts to dress down, she still looked like the expensive trophy wife she was.

Sophie followed her two brothers as they approached their father's ex-wife.

Miranda tucked her keys into the back pocket of her jeans and sighed. "Oh, great, another inquisition."

Kellan ignored her sarcastic comment. "What are you doing here, Miranda?"

Miranda waited for a beat before replying. "I came to check on Blackwood Hollow."

"Aren't you supposed to be living here, as per the terms of the will?" Kellan demanded.

"I'm allowed to leave the property Kellan." Miranda didn't drop his eyes from his. "I had a late night and, probably, too many glasses of champagne at the New Year's Eve party. I wasn't drunk but I was over my limit and, because I am a responsible citizen, I chose to spend the night at The Bellamy." She gestured to the charred ruins. "I was told the stable block and an outbuilding burned down. Any other damage I should know about?"

"Like you actually care." Sophie snorted.

Miranda tapped her foot, obviously exasperated when none of them answered her. "Okay, I'll wake Gage up and get him to give me a status report."

Sophie knew Gage was exhausted and he'd just left, at Kellan's and Clint's insistence, to go home. He needed the rest. She'd stomach answering Miranda's questions if it meant Gage was able to sleep undisturbed.

"The stable block and outbuilding were, as you can see, destroyed. The guest house lost a few rooms but is mostly intact. We lost a lot of grazing land but you have Clint Rockwell to thank that you didn't lose more."

"I'll definitely extend my gratitude to him," Miranda answered, her expression and tone cool. She looked around. "What can I do?"

Three sets of Blackwood eyebrows rose. Vaughn spoke for all of them. "You're going to work?"

"I was planning on it."

"Hauling soggy bricks, trudging through the mud?" Kellan mocked her. "You'll last two seconds."

Miranda bared her teeth at him. "Try me."

Sophie caught the movement of a cameraman heading toward them, intent on capturing their exchange. None of them needed their harsh words to be caught on camera. "Tell your guy to back off, Miranda," she told her, steel in her voice.

Miranda turned and waved the guy away. "Sorry, they are overly inquisitive sometimes and have few boundaries."

"Oh, cut it out, Miranda," Vaughn snapped, sounding irritated. "We all know you are only here, pretending to care about Buck's ranch, as a publicity stunt, to garner more attention for your ridiculously inane show."

"Tell me how you really feel, Vaughn," Miranda murmured, a slight smile tipping up the corners of her mouth.

"They'll film here and they'll edit it to make your ten minutes of work look like you spent the day doing some serious labor. We're not fooled."

"Because nothing gets past you three."

Sophie couldn't decide whether that was sarcasm she heard in Miranda's voice or not. But the calm, smirky smile remained on her face. Miranda's smile widened as she made eye contact with all three of them. "So nice chatting with you all again. It's always a highlight of my day."

Yep, that was definitely sarcasm. Sophie watched her walk away and narrowed her eyes at Miranda's slim back and the cocky sway to her hips.

Oh, Sophie couldn't wait to get to New York City and find the footage she needed to take the bitch down.

Clint appreciated the *Secret Lives* stars' willingness to help with the cleanup of Blackwood Hollow, but honestly, they tended to create more problems than they solved. Lulu, Miranda and Fee, obviously, genuinely helped the process, but the blonde and the sultry brunette spent most of their time gossiping about the fire and chatting up any man with a pulse.

He was over it.

The rain had stopped and the wet ground had killed any embers that could spark into a problematic fire again. He was grateful for the rain, obviously, but now they were clearing waterlogged areas where mud and soot and water mixed together to create a horrible sludge.

He'd been shuttling between Royal and Blackwood Hollow since dawn and on arriving back at Buck's ranch, he found himself in the middle of a Blackwood family argument around the best way to clear the debris of the destroyed buildings.

Vaughn thought the best solution was to bring in backhoes and level the half-collapsed outbuilding and the listing stable. Kellan thought both structures could be shored up.

Both agreed they needed the insurance agent to visit the property before any decision was made.

Neither was thrilled when Miranda Blackwood reminded them that, as the owner, she would make the final decision about how to go forward.

Ugly words were exchanged and Clint walked away, not wanting to get involved in their family dynamics. They needed to work it out themselves, in their own way.

Clint tugged his heavy work gloves into place and

walked back over to the burned-out barn where Fee and Lulu were hauling pieces of wood away to pile them neatly to the side. A cameraman followed their every move and their cast-mate Rafaela watched, her phone in hand.

The day was warmer than expected and his jeans were wet but he refused, like the other guys, to wear shorts. He was hot, uncomfortable and exhausted after he and Fee had spent most of the night burning up the sheets in a lovemaking session as hot as it was intense—a few hours of soul-touching, concentrated, breath-stealing emotion.

It had been magnificent, but today he was at the end of his rope: tired, mentally wiped and physically drained. He was also, he realized, peopled out. He needed to be alone, to soak in some silence, to recharge his batteries. He hadn't spent this much time with this many people since he was in the unit. He was done.

But he had work to do—his neighbor needed help, so did the town, and he would not let them down. He just didn't want to talk to anybody while he worked.

"Clint, how are you feeling this morning?"

Clint turned around at the strange voice and glared when he found a camera in his face. Putting his hand up, he shoved the camera away. "Get that out of my face."

The cameraman took a few steps back but didn't lower the device. "How do you feel about the fires, about the rain, about the mess Royal is in?"

Crap on a cracker. Clint rubbed the back of his

wrist against his forehead to wipe away the perspiration.

"Any comment, Clint?"

Yeah, he had a comment. He looked directly into the camera and spoke with deadly intent. "Yeah, here it is…if you point that thing in my direction one more time, I am going to ram it down your throat. Clear enough?"

The camera lowered and he saw both fear and resentment in Jimmy's eyes. "Just trying to do my job, man."

"Do it somewhere far, far away from me," Clint told him before turning around to lift a piece of corrugated iron off a wooden beam. He walked it over to a pile he'd started and carefully placed it on top of another square piece of iron, trying to ignore the phantom pains shooting from his stump up his leg. It had been months since he'd experienced them and he'd thought they were behind him.

He'd pushed himself too hard and for too long. Clint needed to take a non-opiate painkiller—he had some in the car. Maybe the analgesic would disrupt the false signals his brain was receiving from his nonexistent limb.

He pulled off his gloves and walked toward his car, but before he'd taken a few steps, another camera appeared on the periphery of his vision. "Clint, can you comment on the cleanup?"

He was going to kill someone, he genuinely was. Clint stopped, clenched his fists and counted to ten. Then to twenty. When he thought he had his temper under control, he opened his eyes and nailed the cameraman with a hard look.

Before he had time to issue another threat, he saw Fee hurrying over to him, looking determined. Striding up to the camera, she pulled a jack from its connection and held it in her hand as the camera lowered.

"Vincent, back off. Leave Clint alone."

Vincent looked like he wanted to argue but the fierce look on Fee's face stopped him in his tracks. Fee wiggled her fingers. "Give me your radio."

Vincent dug a small two-way radio out of his back pocket and handed it over, resigned. Fee took the device, hit the button and spoke into the receiver. "This is Seraphina Martinez and I'm ordering you all to stay away from Clint Rockwell."

While he appreciated her intervention, Clint didn't need her to talk for him. He opened his mouth to blast her but a disembodied voice from the radio beat him to it. Clint recognized it as being the director's voice.

"You aren't the boss here, Seraphina. Rockwell is the hero of the hour—we need to get him on screen."

"I distinctly recall Nigel telling us all we shouldn't force cooperation from the Royal residents. Clint wants privacy, and he's entitled to it," Fee shot back.

God, he could fight his own battles. And by making her announcement, they'd attracted the interest of the *Secret Lives* cast, the Blackwood siblings and Kace LeBlanc, who was there, Clint presumed, to help with the cleanup.

"Seraphina, enough! I lost the use of my leg, not

my brain or my mouth," Clint roared and he caught the hurt in Fee's eyes as she turned to face him.

Then a bright red flush climbed up her neck and into her face. Her humiliation was easy to see in her eyes as she said, "I was just trying to help, Clint."

"I don't need your goddamn help. I don't need anybody's help. All I want to do is go to my truck without tripping over a reality TV star or cameraman. I just want fifteen minutes of goddamn peace."

Fee lifted her hand and backed away as she sent him a princess-looking-at-a-peasant look. "Fine. Do what you need to do."

Shit, he'd screwed up. He started to call her back, to say—what? Apologize? Yeah, he could apologize, not for threatening the cameramen but for snapping at her in front of her friends and coworkers.

That had been badly done and he was ashamed of himself.

But Fee was out of hearing distance and his leg was killing him. Before he could make amends, he needed to take some pills and a mental break, calm the hell down. He needed to find a quiet place, maybe do some meditation exercises, to rest his body, his mind and his eyes.

He'd make amends later; right now he needed to be alone.

Clint dug his painkillers from the first aid box he kept in the car and chased them down with half a bottle of water. Walking away from the car, he skirted the damaged building and walked into the surviving stable block, welcoming the quiet shadows within the building. Yay, privacy. He saw a straw bale tucked into a dark corner and, feeling hot and miserable, decided to step out of his wet jeans for a little bit.

Sitting down on the bale, he stretched out his legs in front of him and debated whether to remove his prosthetic. Deciding to leave it on, he rested his head against the cool wall and closed his eyes, breathing deeply to calm his tumultuous brain.

It had been a tough few days but he'd endured many days a great deal worse.

Eighteen hours of fighting fires shouldn't wipe him out.

But it wasn't the fire—not really. No, what did make him feel tired, emotionally displaced and, yeah, terrified, was that he was so close to dropping to his knees—one knee—and begging Seraphina to stay in Royal.

To stay with him.

There, he'd admitted it. He wanted her to stay, on the ranch, with him. Which was, admittedly, crazy. Fee was a city girl, a TV star. She needed to be seen at restaurant openings, in clubs, dancing on bars in bohemian pubs. What could he offer her? He had wealth, sure, but comfort or even luxury couldn't turn Royal into a big, bustling city. She was not a rancher's wife, girlfriend or significant other. Jesus, the woman couldn't even ride a horse.

It didn't matter how unsuited she was to live on a ranch, on his ranch; he still wanted to beg her to stay. But that was a special type of madness.

Because, if she did, what would happen? They

would have great sex for a few weeks, maybe a few months, before the isolation would get to her and she'd start to think she had someplace better to be.

Good sex would fade into dissatisfaction and her fascination with ranch life, with him, would fade too.

He refused to put himself in that position.

But, damn, it was a great dream. And because he was exhausted, and a little sad and a lot overwhelmed, he allowed himself to daydream about her cooking in his kitchen, teaching her to ride, making love to her in the flowers blooming in the high meadow in spring. He dreamed of her in his bed, in his shower...

In his life.

Later Clint realized how exhausted he must have been because he, a highly trained ex-army ranger, never once suspected someone stood in the shadows, watching him.

Eleven

The next day Fee was riding shotgun in one of Rockwell Ranch's pickups and she turned to face Clint as he drove up Blackwood Hollow's long drive. After a brief apology from Clint for his rudeness—which she readily accepted—and a solid night's sleep, he looked better than he had yesterday. He was back to being strong, fit and in control.

She needed to tell him shooting was scheduled to end in two days and she had a plane ticket back to the city that same evening. She wanted to tell him that, if he asked her to stay, she would. How did she tell him he was the only man who could persuade her not to move on, to plant her feet?

The only person she felt safe enough to risk her future on?

Clint had proved himself, over and over. He was steadfast, courageous and honorable.

She should tell him, she had to get the words out. But what if she was reading too much into the situation, seeing possibilities not there? What if he didn't want her...like that? What if he was perfectly happy to see the back of her, to let her go?

What then?

She was driving herself crazy. Either way, one of them had to raise the subject, but seeing the entire cast and crew of *Secret Lives* waiting for them on the steps leading up to Blackwood Hollow's imposing front door, she knew their discussion would be delayed.

Fee wasn't sure whether to laugh or cry, to feel relieved or irritated. God, this falling in love business was hell on the nerves.

Clint parked his car and, seeing the excited faces of her colleagues, turned to her and raised his eyebrows. "What's going on?"

"No idea," Fee said, opening her door and jumping out. It was barely nine and nobody on set usually managed to crack a smile this early. They all needed at least four cups of coffee and a couple more hours before that happened.

Fee looked at Lulu and saw her smile was strained and she wasn't as excited as Rafaela or the producers. Gemma, their PR person, looked like she wanted to jump out of her skin with excitement.

"What's going on?" Fee asked Lulu.

Lulu didn't answer her, she just turned to Gemma and gestured for her to explain.

"Clint's photo has gone viral," Gemma gushed.

Okay, what photo? She didn't know what they were talking about. "Explain."

"Rafaela went around town yesterday, doing a photo essay of Royal, looking for the poignant, pertinent photos, the human-interest angle," Gemma responded.

Human interest? Fee almost snorted. Rafaela wasn't exactly the most empathetic or sensitive of the ex-wives.

The situation would be funny...if there hadn't been mention of a photo of Clint. Fee felt ice invade her veins and, worse, she felt Clint stiffening behind her.

"What photo?" Fee demanded, between clenched teeth. Clint was so publicity averse, any photo of him hitting the tabloids or papers would piss him off. God, she hoped it was from a distance, and flattering.

Gemma waved her tablet around and it took all Fee had not to snatch it from her hands.

"Rafaela posted it to her social media accounts, then we shared it and it's had about half a million retweets and a million views. It's hot." Gemma sent a flirty smile Clint's way that had Fee grinding her teeth.

"Show it to me," Fee demanded.

Gemma held out her iPad and Fee took it, holding her breath. Fee looked down and read the headline first: News Anchor's Son a Local Hero, This Is What True Courage Looks Like.

In the photo, Clint sat on a hay bale, head against the wall, eyes closed. He wore plain black boxer shorts and a sleeveless tank, looking hot and sexy and dirty. He appeared utterly exhausted but a small smile played around his mouth and there was a hint of pride and satisfaction on his face.

It was a powerful photograph, soul gripping and intensely emotional, and she could see why it had gone viral. Clint looked like the hero he was.

Fee heard his sharp intake of air and immediately the atmosphere changed. She closed her eyes and waited for his explosion, for his temper to ignite. She instantly knew why he was upset—he never allowed anyone to see his prosthetic leg. He was intensely private and his disability was an off-limits subject.

But Rafaela had exposed him, showing what he tried to keep hidden from the world.

Fee turned around slowly and when she met his eyes, she saw the betrayal in his eyes, the sharp kick of shock. Then his expression turned bleak and she felt him slipping away from her.

Fee felt Lulu remove the tablet from her shaking fingers and felt her friend's hand on her back, steadying her.

Oh, God, this was bad.

This was so, so bad. Clint ignored her beseeching look and regarded her as if she were a brown recluse spider he'd found on his shoe. "Excellent work,

Martinez. Fantastic publicity. Glad it all worked out for you."

Oh, no, now that was unfair. She didn't know anything about the photograph and she wouldn't be blamed for it. "I would've killed it if I'd known it would be used—or if I'd known she'd taken it in the first place."

"It's a great photo," Rafaela protested, "and it's very inspirational."

"Take it down," Clint told Gemma, whose excitement had turned to confusion. *"Now."*

Gemma exchanged a panicked look with Miranda. "I can take it down from our site but it's already out there on social media. Hundreds of thousands of people have reposted the picture, the news outlets have picked it up and interviewed the residents of Royal, who have nothing but amazing things to say about you."

She got increasingly flustered when Clint's face took on that robotic expression Fee so hated.

"I don't understand why you are mad," Gemma wailed.

"And I have no intention of explaining," Clint said, his voice a few degrees lower than freezing point. He turned his attention to Miranda. "I'm done. This stops, now…today. Either they leave or I do."

"Clint, don't do this," Miranda said, her voice soothing. "I understand you are angry, and it is a shocking invasion of your privacy, but maybe you should take a few days to cool down before you do or say something you'll regret."

Clint folded his arms and nailed her with a frigid look. "Either you get rid of them or I walk. That means no one will be around to oversee the lands, the cleanup, your hands, the stock."

Miranda held his eyes for ten seconds before nodding. She turned to the director and lifted her hand, dragging it across her throat. "We're done. Let's go."

"But I have a schedule! There are shots, interviews—"

Miranda narrowed her eyes. "I said...we're done."

Miranda told the crew and Fee's costars to head for their cars. Lulu gripped her hand and squeezed before walking away.

Clint jerked his head to Miranda. "You're going to miss your lift back to town," he told Fee.

Fee felt her anger bubble, way down deep in her stomach. "You know I'm not going to walk away without discussing this."

"I have nothing to say to you, Seraphina."

God, he'd never said her name in such a dismissive way, like he had acid on his tongue. "I did not know anything about the photograph, Clint."

"You're an integral part of the show. Are you seriously telling me nobody told you they were going to plaster a photograph of your disabled lover on social media? Please, tell me another lie! I dare you."

"Nobody told me." Fee lifted her hand when he started to interrupt her. "Maybe they didn't think they needed to because they saw what I did."

"Yeah, a goddamn cripple."

Fee grabbed his arm, trying not to feel hurt when

he shook off her touch. "They saw a guy who went above and beyond the call of duty, who worked like a Trojan to make sure his community was safe, who still went to work the day after that grueling day. I saw a guy who can do everything a guy with two legs can do, and more. I saw a hot, sexy, tired guy who looked amazing."

"Bullshit, Seraphina. Stop trying to spin this!"

She was so over him putting himself down. "*You* stop! Stop assuming everyone is judging you. The only person who sees you as being disabled is you, Clint. You! No one else!"

Sparks of pure silver anger flashed in Clint's eyes. "Quit blowing smoke up my ass, Martinez. I know most women see me as only half a man. There's nothing I can do to make myself whole." He was just making her angrier and angrier.

Instead of yelling at him, Fee folded her arms and waited for him to look at her. "Are you done with the pity party?"

"What?"

She ignored the roar that had horses in the nearby paddock lifting their heads. "When you are done feeling sorry yourself, I have something to say."

"I'm not interested," Clint snapped back.

"You have yelled at me, embarrassed me in front of my friends and made a ton of assumptions that simply aren't true. You owe me the right to speak."

Clint hauled in a deep breath and she watched his big chest rise and fall. When she knew she had his attention, she pushed her words past her teeth.

"Fact, you have one leg. Fact, you are technically disabled. Fact, you lost your leg in an act of supreme bravery. Fact, your mother is a stone-cold bitch and those women you hooked up with who rejected you? Shallow and superficial. And how dare you compare what they said or did to me?"

Fee drilled a hole into his chest with her finger. "I am rude and loud-mouthed and outspoken but I am not fake, Rockwell, and that's what you're accusing me of being. I made love to you because I think you are the most amazing, inspiring, capable guy I've ever met. So, once again, the only person in the whole goddamn world who has an issue with you missing a limb is you."

"And my mother, and those women—"

"Again, superficial and shallow. Why are you even giving them headspace? I'm standing here telling you your town loves you, that I do too, and the people you are listening to are people who have proved themselves to be douches. What is wrong with *you*?"

"I hate that photo—it makes me look weak!"

"You look strong and brave."

Clint shook his head and Fee realized she was fighting a lost cause. She couldn't change his mind for him. He had to realize his worth, for himself, by himself. She held up her hand and blew air into her cheeks.

"I'm crazy about you Clint, head over heels in love with you, but I can't be with you. I can't spend the rest of my life reassuring you of your worth. I'm a strong woman. I need a man who's equally aware of his strength. Until you can accept yourself, love yourself, exactly as you are, as I do, I'm wasting my time."

Clint stared at her, obviously shocked by her honesty.

"I'm going back to New York, as soon as I can. This was fun but now it's not."

Clint nodded once. His short, sharp gesture was an exclamation point at the end of their conversation. "I think that's a very good idea. Even if I believed you about not being half a man—and I don't—we could never work. You're town, I'm country. We're exact opposites."

Fee felt like her heart was breaking but she forced a smile onto her face. She placed her hand on his chest and felt him stiffen as she leaned into him, felt him pull back as she lifted herself onto her heels to speak in his ear.

"Coward. You can face down a band of terrorists intent on killing you and your team but you can't let people see your leg, you can't love me? Shame on you, Rockwell."

Fee was close to crying, but she refused to allow him to see her tears so she quickly turned and headed for the driveway, hoping against hope Lulu was waiting for her, that she wouldn't have to phone for a ride, leaving her waiting here with the gorgeous, broken man she loved with every fiber of her being.

Through her tears Fee saw her best friend sitting in the driver's seat of her rented Jeep, far enough away not to hear her conversation but close enough to intervene if their fight went south.

God bless her best friend, Fee thought as she slid into the passenger and burst into tears.

Lulu, because she was a goddess, just held her hand and let her weep before driving her back to a life she no longer wanted.

Twelve

Two weeks passed before Clint made a trip into Royal, and only because it was the grand opening of the new fire station. He'd dressed in a sharp white button-down shirt, a tie and black chinos, and desperately wished he was in his jeans and boots, and on one of his many horses. Or working on Tim's truck, having recently received the Chevy back from the body shop. He did not want to smile and shake hands with the Royal residents, to face their sympathetic and prying eyes, answer his questions about how he was doing.

He was alone. He was fine…

Which was all a steaming pile of bull crap.

He was alone but he wasn't fine, he was just holding on.

Ignoring the cars parked in the front of the building, Clint skirted around to the parking area at the
back and slid his SUV between the two new, state-
of-the-art fire engines he'd donated. The firefighting/
rescue helicopters were parked at the regional air-
port, ready to be dispatched at a moment's notice. He
had provided funds for two teams of permanent firefighters, a trained medic and a pilot, saying he would
serve as backup to fly as and when he was needed.

He was giving back to his community—it was
all he could do.

Clint exited his car, feeling like ants were crawl-
ing under his skin. He couldn't go anywhere in Royal
without thinking about Fee and that, frankly, pissed
him off. And he couldn't decide what he was most
angry about—the invasion of his privacy or Fee lying
to him by telling him she loved him…

Oh, wait, maybe it was the fact she'd called him
a goddamn *coward*.

He'd snuck behind enemy lines in the dead of
night, risked his skin a thousand times, suffered de-
privations and starvation rations, endured mortar
strikes and enemy fire, he'd earned medals—a goddamn Purple Heart!—and yet she'd still thrown the
insult straight in his face.

How dare she judge him?

Walking into the large empty bay where the cater-
ing staff was setting up tables for drinks and food,
he ran up the flight of stairs into the commander's
office, hoping to hide out until he was needed. He'd

say a few words and then fade away; nobody would even miss him.

Clint threw himself into the leather office chair behind the desk and rested his forearms on his thighs, staring down at the hard-wearing floor beneath his feet. His thoughts, as they always did, turned back to Fee. What she'd said was unforgivable, hurtful, cruel. This—this was why he should avoid relationships.

Because they sucked, dammit.

Well, like rehab and surgery and PTSD and everything else he'd endured, it was over and he could put it behind him. He had work to do, a ranch to run, the fire station to oversee. All of that would keep him sane. He'd launch the fire station, and after it was up and running, he'd retreat and lick his wounds.

He'd tried, and failed, at a relationship. He should learn from it and move on.

Clint heard the sharp rap on his door and lifted his head to see Jeff, the about-to-be-appointed fire chief, standing in the doorway. Clint stood up and gestured to the chair. "Sorry, I should've asked you if I could be in here."

"Clint, you paid for everything here. You can be anywhere you like. And I don't have secrets to hide."

Clint sent him a tight smile and took a surreptitious look at his watch. The function wasn't supposed to start for another half hour so he walked over to the window and stared down at the cars streaming into the parking lot.

Damn, too many people…

Jeff sat down on the edge of his desk and picked

up a signed baseball. "So, you must be pleased with the response you received from the photograph."

Yeah, *thrilled*. Not.

"I read a lot of the comments and the responses. Not sure how much of it you've seen, but hell, if it was me, I'd be floating near the ceiling," Jeff commented.

Clint frowned, confused. "What are you talking about?"

"Thousands of vets and paraplegics and disabled people—women, children and men—left comments saying you are a role model, an inspiration, and that you've given them hope. The story was picked up by a national news outlet and you're trending. God, your social media accounts must be blowing up."

He didn't have any social media accounts so he'd had no idea of the extent of the reach of the photograph. "And the responses were mostly positive?" he asked, confused.

"They were *all* positive. You're the new poster boy for true American grit. And your mom has been hitting the radio stations and interview circuits, boasting about you and the fact she taught you everything you know."

She wished. And how typical it was for his mom to jump on the publicity he generated. But none of it mattered, not really, because he'd lost the person he loved.

It meant little without her.

"Talking about being an inspiration," Jeff said,

"would you do me a favor and meet someone? He's in the gym."

Clint started to shake his head but Jeff held up his hand. "Ten minutes, Clint. Please?"

He didn't want to. He wanted to stay here and enjoy his solitude. *Coward,* a little voice inside him stated. It sounded like Fee.

Wanting to be alone wasn't an act of cowardice. *Sure it is...*

Annoyed by the direction of his thoughts, Clint nodded abruptly and followed Jeff out of his office and down a floor to the gym the architects had tucked into the corner of the fire station. Clint had requested the workout room for the firefighters but had also suggested that it could be used by any veterans in the area who couldn't afford the fees at a normal fitness center.

Jeff was fully on board with his idea.

When Clint stepped into the gym, he saw a kid standing in the middle of the floor, his hand on a thick rope dangling from the ceiling. He sported a mop of bright blond hair but Clint's attention was immediately captured by his prosthetic leg.

Clint started to back away and hit Jeff's broad, solid chest.

"He's eleven years old, he's a cancer survivor and all he wants is to meet you. He won't say why or how you landed on his radar, but he's obsessed with you. His mom, a waitress, took a day off work to bring him here when they found out you'd be at the ceremony today. Apparently, it's the most excited she's seen him in months."

Clint felt Jeff's hand on his shoulder and his fingers dig into his skin. "You will not mess this day up for him, Clint."

Well, okay then.

Clint looked around and saw the boy's mom standing against the far wall, looking anxious. She also looked too thin and way too tired. A single mom, he realized, trying to cope as best she could with a kid who'd suffered through a horrible disease and was now physically challenged.

Sucked...

Clint jammed his hands into the pockets of his chinos and walked into the center of the gym, sighing when anxious bright-blue eyes met his. He held out his hand and waited for the kid to put his much smaller hand in his before giving it a gentle shake. "Hey, bud, I'm Clint."

"I'm Beck."

"I heard you wanted to speak to me."

Beck folded his arms across his chest and tipped his head to one side. "I've read every article about you and there were a lot."

Clint heard the challenging note in his voice and considered apologizing. If there were as many articles and comments about him as Jeff said, then the kid had spent a hell of a lot of his time reading.

Clint just held his gaze and lifted an eyebrow, waiting for Beck to continue.

"Did you really fight off terrorists by yourself, with half your leg missing?" Beck demanded.

Since he wasn't about to glamorize war, Clint just nodded. "If I hadn't, they would've killed me and my team."

"And they cut off your leg afterward?"

"They did."

"Were you mad?"

Out of the corner of his eye, he saw Beck's mother step forward and he held up his hand, telling her he had this. "At losing my leg? Sure I was. It was a shitty thing to happen."

Maybe he should apologize for his language but after enduring cancer and losing his leg, he was sure the kid could cope with some swearing.

"But you learned how to walk, to run, to ride a horse, to become a helicopter pilot with one leg."

"I did."

"How?" Beck looked at the rope in his hand and gave it a tug. "How did you know you could do it?"

"I didn't," Clint replied, keeping it honest. "But I knew I had to try. That trying and failing was better than not trying at all."

Beck shook his head. "I don't want to fail."

"Sometimes you do fail, that's life. But you have to give it your best shot. Not trying is being a coward and being a coward isn't something a soldier can be."

You had to give it your best shot. And he hadn't tried with Fee and, ergo, he *was* a coward.

Shit.

Of all the times to realize she was right and he

was wrong. Clint ran a hand over his face and mentally released a stream of F-bombs. Saying them aloud would be more satisfying, but right now, he had a kid who was looking at him like he hung the moon, like he had all the answers to every question Beck had ever had.

A kid who was hurt, badly bruised and insecure.

He needed to restore some of Beck's confidence and he needed to do it right now. Clint held up his finger and told Beck to stay put. Motioning Jeff over, he asked whether he could loan him some gear. He changed into a Royal Fire Department T-shirt, a pair of exercise shorts and running shoes, grateful he and Jeff were roughly the same size. He looked down at his bare prosthetic and shrugged off the wave of panic. If a kid could show the world his leg, Clint could too.

He jogged back into the gym and easily pulled himself up the dangling rope until he was close to the ceiling. He hung there for a sec, before sliding down and landing lightly on his feet.

He held the rope out to Beck. "Your turn."

"I can't. I don't know how. I only have one leg."

"You have just as many legs as me, and you won't know if you can do it until you try. One hand over the other, pull. Then wind the rope around your leg and pull up again."

Beck managed to pull himself up a few feet and grinned down at Clint, joy on his face. Clint high-fived him, then helped him down. "Twenty push-ups, soldier."

Beck sent him an uncertain look but copied Clint's stance, his toothpick arms managing five push-ups to Clint's quick twenty before he collapsed, his forehead on the floor. "I'm so bad at this."

"But are you trying?"

Beck turned his face. "Yeah, I am."

"I'm not asking you to be great at it. I'm asking you to try."

Clint worked with him for the next half hour, making Beck lift ropes, flip tires, practice squats and planks, vaguely aware he'd gathered an audience but keeping his sole attention on Beck. The kid's face was red and his hair was damp with sweat by the time he finished but his face radiated a sense of achievement and, yeah, pride.

Clint handed him a towel and a bottle of water and sat down next to him on a bench. "The kids at school, they call me a crip and a gimp," Beck told him, his voice soft.

Clint silently cursed at kids' cruelty. "Screw 'em. Work to be better than them and kick their asses when you're done. But don't tell your mom I said that."

Beck looked over to where his mom stood, talking to an olive-skinned brunette dressed in a flame-orange minidress and black knee-high boots.

She had her back to him, but he knew that body from any angle. Besides, only one person would have the audacity, the balls, to wear such a sexy pair of boots in Royal and look amazing doing it.

Clint raised his bottle to his lips, his heart stuttering. Fee was back.

Fee. Was. Back...

"Would you teach me to kick their asses? To defend myself?"

It took all he had to pull his attention back to Beck. "I'll talk to your mom, see if we can get you up here once or twice a month for some training, some lessons."

Clint darted another look at Fee and turned back to his new friend. "Look, Beck, I want you to remember you are allowed to fail, you're allowed to not be good at something—"

"What aren't you good at?" Beck interjected, his eyes bright with curiosity.

Clint didn't hesitate. "Dealing with people, checking my pride, allowing people in, being thoughtful toward the ones who matter to me. So, hug your mom, bud, I think she needs it now and again."

Beck nodded solemnly.

"I was saying you are allowed not to be good at something but you have to try. Promise me you will always try."

Beck tipped his head to the side. "Are you going to try with people?"

Clint grinned. "Touché, kid."

Yeah, he was going to try. And he was going to start with Fee.

Beck wrinkled his nose. "I don't know what that means."

Clint ruffled his hair and stood up. "It means you turned the tables on me."

He nodded toward the locker room. "Good job, bud. Go wash your face and hands."

Clint waited for Beck outside the locker room, thinking he hadn't even broken a sweat. He could go back in, change back into his clothes and carry on with his day. But he didn't want to waste a minute so when Beck walked out of the locker room, Clint placed his hand on the kid's shoulder and walked him back over to his teary-eyed mom. Fee gave Clint a brief nod of greeting and, being Fee and outgoing, immediately engaged Beck in conversation.

Beck's mom—she introduced herself as Jan—placed her hand on his arm. "Thank you for giving him your time. He's been struggling lately—he's been very sullen and uncommunicative. I haven't been able to talk to him for months and the only time he's really spoken to me was to ask to come see you."

Uncomfortable with her praise and thanks, Clint asked for her cell phone. Taking it, he programmed in his number and told Jan to call him when Beck was acting up. Or whenever she or Beck needed to talk.

Tears streamed down Jan's face. Fee handed her a tissue and she wiped her eyes as she turned her attention to her son.

"Did you see me, Mom? Did you see what I did? Clint said I have to try."

Clint watched them walk out of the now-empty gym and turned back to his biggest problem and his greatest joy. He didn't know what to say so he went for the obvious.

"I didn't expect to see you back in Royal, Fee." He looked past her, looking for the cameras. "I presume your crew is outside, filming this opening of the fire station. It's supposed to be more of an appreciation party for the volunteer firefighters, but we decided to hold both functions at once—"

"My crew isn't here," Fee interrupted him.

Clint frowned, puzzled. "I would've thought they would want to be here. It's a nice ending to the story."

"Since I'm leaving the show, I'm not part of the decision-making." She wrinkled her nose and Clint realized he wanted to watch her do that for the rest of his life. Could he ask her to give him another chance? What if he failed?

But he had to take his own advice.

But before he threw himself off a cliff, he wanted some more facts. "What, exactly, do you mean by that?"

"It means I am quitting the show," Fee told him, her tone still cool. "I still have to negotiate my exit, but I've made up my mind. I only came by today to tell you I've decided Royal is my town and I need to be here. I'm sorry if that doesn't suit you but Royal suits me."

Wait…what? What the hell?

"I'm sorry, what did you say?"

"I'm renting a cottage in Royal, working on a cookbook and I have feelers out to do a cooking show." She shrugged her slim shoulders. "Eventually I'll either buy or build a place but I felt I owed it to you to tell you I'm back. I'm not asking, or expecting, a damn thing from you."

Clint cocked his head. "Well, damn, now that's a pity."

Fee's eyes turned a shade of bitter chocolate. "You should also know I have no intention of climbing into your bed and being tossed out when you tire of me. Or when you get scared."

Fair point. "What if I just keep you in my bed, in my house, in my life for the rest of my life?"

Fee closed her eyes, color receding from her face. "That's such a cruel thing to say, Clint. You've been an ass and a jerk, but you were never once cruel. Congratulations, lieutenant, you've reached a new low."

Fee turned to walk away and Clint stared at her back, completely confused. He'd just tossed his heart at her feet and she thought he was taunting her by offering something he didn't intend to deliver? Yeah, he really, really, really needed to work on his communication skills. He might never be good at it but there was a lot of room for improvement.

"I missed you."

Fee stopped in her tracks and he heard her loud sigh. She started to walk again and he threw another truth her way. "You were right. I *am* a coward."

Oh, God, that hurt, but then the truth always did. Fee stopped again, slowly turned around and raised one dark eyebrow. "Sure, when it comes to me."

Typical Fee, never one to give an inch. But at least

she wasn't walking away. She kept her eyes on him as she said, "But please, feel free to tell me how you came to that conclusion."

Sarcastic as well. He loved it. Loved her. "I worked my ass off to be capable, to show the world I could do anything I did before and more. But I didn't work at relationships and I didn't bother to work out how to deal with people. Because people are complicated, contrary, and they don't always react the way you want them to."

"We don't all jump when you bark an order, lieutenant."

He ignored her sarcasm. "So, I withdrew. I've always been solitary, Fee, always a loner. My ex, those women, their…insensitivity and my mother's comments about my disability, gave me the excuse I needed to not try, to not interact. It took a fast-talking, sexy, mouthy reality TV star to show me I'd stopped trying with people. That, when it came to relationships, I'm a coward." Clint shook his head. "It was a truth I didn't want to acknowledge."

Fee nodded. When Clint didn't say anything more, she lifted her hands before pointing to the door. "I'm going to go and I think people want to get this show on the road. James Harrison probably wants to get the formalities over with so he can have a beer."

"The president of the TCC can wait," Clint told her. "I'm not done."

"I don't know what there's left to say," Fee admitted.

Clint walked over to her and gently lifted a tendril off her cheek and tucked it behind her ear. "Oh, I have quite a bit still to say."

He saw the trepidation and the faint flicker of hope in her eyes. "Since when did you get to be Mr. Chatty?"

"Since I looked up and saw you across the room and I knew there was no way I was going to let you leave my life again." His fingers brushed her ear, ran down her neck, and he felt her shudder. "I wasn't joking earlier...stay in my house, stay in my life."

"Clint..." Fee begged him but he wasn't sure what she was asking.

So he kept talking. "I'm completely utterly, crazily in love with you, Seraphina. You brought color and warmth and a fair amount of craziness into my life and I don't want to go back to that colorless world again."

Fee's eyes glistened with tears and she finally, finally touched him by placing her hand on his heart. "Do you mean that?"

"Those few, inadequate words don't even begin to cover the depth of my love for you." Clint cupped her beautiful face. "You just told me you are staying here, that this is your town. But did you mean it? Is this really where you want to be?"

"Why are you asking?" Fee asked, tipping her head.

"I don't want you to settle, just because I am here. I want you to be happy and if you're not going to be happy in Royal, then we'll find another place, any place." He shrugged. "I might have to buy a plane so I can come back regularly to keep an eye on the ranch but we can live anywhere."

"And you'd go with me?" Fee asked, a smile pulling her mouth up.

She was where he needed to be. Yeah, he'd miss his ranch but they'd make it work. "As long as you are happy," Clint murmured. "Making you happy is all I care about, Fee."

And it was. His life was now hers. Her happiness was everything.

"That's the sweetest thing anyone has ever said to me," Fee stated, looping her arms around his neck. "But might I remind you of one salient point you seem to have forgotten, Rockwell?"

"What's that?"

"I came back to Royal with no expectation of a relationship with you. I came back because I like this town, I like the people and I want to be part of this community. I want to live here, even though I thought I had no chance of being a part of your life."

"Oh." He was struggling to catch up, to make sense of all of this, mostly because Fee was back and in his arms. "So, you're happy to move into my place?"

"More than," Fee said, her thumbs rubbing his jaw. "Tell me you love me before you kiss me senseless, Rockwell."

"Love you, sweetheart."

"Love you back, cowboy," Fee murmured against his lips, but before he could follow through on her command to kiss her senseless, he heard Jeff clearing his throat.

Jeff just grinned when Clint raised his head and gave him a piss-off-I'm-busy glare.

"James is chomping to get started since all the VIPs are present and accounted for."

Fee stepped back from him and Clint groaned his frustration. She slid her hand into his. "We can pick this up later, Clint." She rubbed his T-shirt between her fingers. "You need to change, darling."

Clint looked down at his exercise shorts and his faded T-shirt. Shrugging, he sent Jeff a wry grin. "Tell James I'm changing. I'll be there in five minutes."

Jeff nodded and left, but instead of heading toward the locker room, Clint pulled Fee back into his arms. "Now, where were we?"

"You're not going to change?" Fee asked him.

"I'd rather kiss you." Clint's mouth curved against hers. "Besides, it seems like the whole world has seen my leg and the planet didn't tilt off its axis."

Fee laughed and slapped her mouth against his.

And it was a good fifteen minutes before they made an appearance at the ceremony.

Epilogue

Fee looked at Clint posing for photographs with the mayor of Royal, Jeff, the new fire chief, and James Harrison, the president of the Texas Cattleman's Club, thinking Clint looked perfect in his exercise shorts and the tight fitting Royal FD T-shirt. Yeah, he should be more smartly dressed for such an important occasion, but most of the attendees had heard about his impromptu gym session with young Beck and applauded him for it.

Her man could walk down the main street of Royal buck naked and nobody would blink an eye. He was their own homegrown hero, one of their favorite sons and he could do no wrong.

When it came to her, though…well, she'd seen

firsthand the challenges that faced anyone who loved this man.

Fee didn't have many stars in her eyes, and while she loved him with every strand of DNA she possessed, she wasn't naive enough to believe Life had just sprinkled a can of fairy dust over their lives. She fully accepted that, going forward, there would be problems and arguments and flared tempers and hurt feelings. That was just life. But there'd be love too. Happiness. Passion. Acceptance.

She'd found her happy place and it was here, in Royal, with Clint. And she'd told him the truth earlier. Even if Clint hadn't been part of the deal, she'd want to spend most of her time in Royal, make this town her home base. She felt at ease here, settled.

Royal was where the rest of her life began.

Having finished with the photographer, Clint made a beeline toward her, his hazel eyes more gold than green.

"You okay? Any second thoughts?" he teased, but Fee wasn't fooled by his light tone. He was worried and she couldn't blame him; this happiness was so new, it felt like it might disappear in a puff of smoke.

"Just catching my breath." Fee linked her fingers with his and rested her head on his shoulder, smiling when he dropped a kiss on her hair.

"I know. I keep feeling it's the most amazing dream and I'm going to wake up alone."

Clint took her glass from her hand and placed his mouth over the lipstick mark she'd left on the glass. He swallowed the rest of the chardonnay and handed the glass back to the waitress. He looked around and sent her a conspiratorial grin. "When can we leave? While I'm loving your dress, I sure as hell can't wait to get you out of it."

Fee grinned back. "Rockwell, really? We have to stay for a little while—it'll be rude to leave now."

"Ten minutes? Fifteen?" Clint asked, mischief in his eyes.

Fee rolled her eyes then allowed them to drift around the room, searching for a neutral subject to distract them from what they were both desperate to do. Soon...

"How are the cleanup operations going?"

"Slowly," Clint replied. "There's so much damage, Fee. More buildings were affected than we originally suspected, including the TCC clubhouse. By the way, James Harrison has asked me to join the Texas Cattleman's Club."

That didn't surprise her. "Of course he has. You're the town's hero."

"I wish everyone would stop calling me that. I just did what I needed to do," Clint replied, frustration in his voice. "I was able to help so I did."

He didn't realize many people wouldn't have, that lots of people threw money at a problem and then washed their hands of any responsibility, looking to others to find a solution. Clint used his money, and his time and his skills, and that was a rare and beautiful thing. But she liked the fact he was unaware of just how amazing he was.

"I'm surprised the Blackwood siblings aren't here," Fee commented, changing the subject.

"I heard Sophie Blackwood has left Royal for New York City." Clint shrugged. "Kellan is in Nashville, I think. I'm not sure where Vaughn is at present."

"Kace is here." Fee gestured to the lanky lawyer talking to James Harrison.

"And your friend isn't," Clint said. "Something happening between them?"

Fee was curious on that point too—but Lu had been uncharacteristically quiet lately. Then again, she'd been heartbroken and not really interested in anything but her own misery.

"I don't know. But I haven't been a great friend lately. I've been rather wrapped up in my own heartbreak," she admitted.

Clint turned her to face him and placed his hands on her shoulder. "Hell, Fee, I have to apologize. Again. I acted like a jerk, and I'm really sorry."

"And I was a lot meaner than I needed to be but I was hurt. I'm sorry too. You're not a coward, Clint. I'm so sorry I insulted you like that," Fee said, her heart in her throat. She was still ashamed of herself, that of everything she could've said, she'd gone straight for his emotional jugular.

"But I was. When it came to you, and love, I was a total coward." Clint jerked his head at Beck, who stood by the table laden with desserts, stuffing his mouth. "I told him he had to try, that he could fail but he *had* to try. Then I realized I was crap at taking my own advice. And I looked up and there you were."

He smiled and Fee's heart jumped into her throat. Clint had an amazing smile and she was going to look at it for the rest of her life. How lucky was she?

"Your arrival damn near gave me a heart attack," Clint admitted. He looked at Beck and lifted one huge shoulder. "The fire station project is, obviously, over and we need to clean up Royal but—"

"But?" Fee asked, intrigued by the light she saw in his eyes.

"But I was thinking that, for my next project, I'd like to build a rehab center, a gym, something specifically designed for veterans and people struggling to come to terms with their disabilities. Maybe hire some physios, some counselors, have some skills training. A place of…acceptance."

Fee blinked away her tears. Oh God, that sounded perfect. "It sounds awesome, darling. You'll have my full support, Clint."

"Maybe we can call it Fee's Place, because you led me to a place of acceptance."

She was touched but…no.

"We'll find a name, a good name, but not that one." Fee rested her forehead on his chest before looking up at him, tears rolling down her face. "I'm so in love with you, Rockwell."

"As I am with you," Clint told her, spearing his fingers into her hair and tipping her jaw up to receive his kiss. "I only have one more thing to ask you…"

Oh God, it was too soon. What would she say?

Yes, of course, but were they rushing things? Was she ready for a proposal?

"What?" Fee asked him, sounding a little breathless.

"Can we go home now?"

Fee released a long breath, a little disappointed. "Yeah, sure."

Clint took her hand and led her through the throngs of people, adroitly avoiding everyone who wanted to talk to them by telling them he'd catch up with them soon. Outside, in the cool evening air, he turned back to Fee and smiled at her. "So, would you have said yes?"

She didn't pretend to misunderstand him. "It's very soon but...yes. I would have said yes."

Clint brushed his lips across hers. "Good to know. Let's go home, my darling Fee."

She was already there. No matter where she was, if her hand was in his, she was home.

* * * * *

AVAILABLE THIS MONTH FROM
Harlequin® Desire

FROM BOARDROOM TO BEDROOM
Texas Cattleman's Club: Inheritance • by Jules Bennett

Sophie Blackwood needs the truth to take back what rightfully belongs to her family. Working for media CEO Nigel Townshend is the way to do it. What she doesn't expect is their undeniable attraction. Will her feelings for her British playboy boss derail everything?

BLAME IT ON THE BILLIONAIRE
Blackout Billionaires • by Naima Simone

Nadia Jordan certainly didn't plan on spending the night with Grayson Chandler during the blackout, but the bigger surprise comes when he introduces her as his fake fiancée to avoid his family's matchmaking! But even a fake relationship can't hide their real chemistry...

RULE BREAKER
Dynasties: Mesa Falls • by Joanne Rock

Despite his bad-boy persona, Mesa Falls ranch owner Weston Rivera takes his job very seriously—a point he makes clear to meddlesome financial investigator April Stephens. Stranded together by a storm, their attraction is searing, but can it withstand their differences once the snow clears?

ONE LITTLE INDISCRETION
Murphy International • by Joss Wood

After their night of passion, auction house CEO Carrick Murphy and art detective Sadie Slade aren't looking for anything more. But when she learns she's pregnant, they must overcome their troubled pasts for a chance at lasting happiness...

HIS FORBIDDEN KISS
Kiss and Tell • by Jessica Lemmon

Heiress Taylor Thompson never imagined her night would end with kissing a mysterious stranger—let alone her reluctant date's older brother, Royce Knox! Their spark can't be denied, but will family and professional pressure keep them to just one kiss?

TEMPORARY WIFE TEMPTATION
The Heirs of Hansol • by Jayci Lee

To keep his role as CEO, Garrett Song needs to find a bride, and fast. And Natalie Sobol is the perfect candidate. But their marriage of convenience is rocked when real passion takes over. Can a bargain that was only supposed to be temporary last forever?

Get 4 FREE REWARDS!

We'll send you 2 FREE Books plus 2 FREE Mystery Gifts.

Harlequin® Desire books feature heroes who have it all: wealth, status, incredible good looks... everything but the right woman.

FREE
Value Over
$20

YES! Please send me 2 FREE Harlequin® Desire novels and my 2 FREE gifts (gifts are worth about $10 retail). After receiving them, if I don't wish to receive any more books, I can return the shipping statement marked "cancel." If I don't cancel, I will receive 6 brand-new novels every month and be billed just $4.55 per book in the U.S. or $5.24 per book in Canada. That's a savings of at least 13% off the cover price! It's quite a bargain! Shipping and handling is just 50¢ per book in the U.S. and $1.25 per book in Canada.* I understand that accepting the 2 free books and gifts places me under no obligation to buy anything. I can always return a shipment and cancel at any time. The free books and gifts are mine to keep no matter what I decide.

225/326 HDN GNND

Name (please print)

Address   Apt. #

City   State/Province   Zip/Postal Code

Mail to the Reader Service:
IN U.S.A.: P.O. Box 1341, Buffalo, NY 14240-8531
IN CANADA: P.O. Box 603, Fort Erie, Ontario L2A 5X3

Want to try 2 free books from another series? Call 1-800-873-8635 or visit www.ReaderService.com.

---

*Terms and prices subject to change without notice. Prices do not include sales taxes, which will be charged (if applicable) based on your state or country of residence. Canadian residents will be charged applicable taxes. Offer not valid in Quebec. This offer is limited to one order per household. Books received may not be as shown. Not valid for current subscribers to Harlequin Desire books. All orders subject to approval. Credit or debit balances in a customer's account(s) may be offset by any other outstanding balance owed by or to the customer. Please allow 4 to 6 weeks for delivery. Offer available while quantities last.

Your Privacy—The Reader Service is committed to protecting your privacy. Our Privacy Policy is available online at www.ReaderService.com or upon request from the Reader Service. We make a portion of our mailing list available to reputable third parties that offer products we believe may interest you. If you prefer that we not exchange your name with third parties, or if you wish to clarify or modify your communication preferences, please visit us at www.ReaderService.com/consumerchoice or write to us at Reader Service Preference Service, P.O. Box 9062, Buffalo, NY 14240-9062. Include your complete name and address.

HD20

Love Harlequin romance?

DISCOVER.

Be the first to find out about promotions,
news and exclusive content!

EXPLORE.

Sign up for the Harlequin e-newsletter and
download a free book from any series at
TryHarlequin.com.

CONNECT.

Join our Harlequin community to share
your thoughts and connect with other
romance readers!
Facebook.com/groups/HarlequinConnection

**ROMANCE WHEN
YOU NEED IT**

HSOCIAL2018